RANDY AND LARRY
SORT OF SAVE
THE WORLD

Brent McLean

To Nat, Mat, and Bat, with love.

PART 1: DOWN THE RABBIT HOLE

1. THE FORCE EXPOSES

"Forced exposition," Larry said.

"Right," said Randy. "So that's, like, when you use your characters to explain elements of your story through dialogue that seems awkward or unnatural to the reader."

Larry nodded. "Often because the characters are saying things that they all know already. Oh, hey. Speaking of forced, remember when you forced me to take this stupid writing class?"

"I didn't *force* you, I just said it might be fun."

"Well, it isn't," said Larry, glancing wistfully out the window at the cloudless blue sky reflected in a shimmering sea of steel and glass skyscrapers. "Hey, there's something we both already know."

"And you're telling me this," Randy said, rolling his eyes slightly, "because our teacher Judy is having us practice her trademarked Eight Elements of Bad Writing, so that we can get a sense of how they feel. Today's element is Unnatural Dialogue, and our exercise is on forced exposition, so we've broken out into groups and we're forced expos... exposit... expositioning? To each other."

"Look," said Larry. "As you may know, you and I live in New York City, which means there's absolutely no need for us to sit around and write about people we don't know doing things, when we could be the ones actually doing things! Plus, you've already found a girl you like in the class. Why don't I just go home now, and you can keep forced exposing yourself to her."

"They're called *women*," Randy sighed.

"And it's *expositing*, and also I'm right here, you guys," Kelli added. "As you are no doubt already aware, Judy broke us out into groups of three for this exercise."

"And she's right here," agreed Randy. "Plus that wasn't even forced exposition, because she didn't already know that. Asshole."

"Yeah, I kind of knew that," Kelli laughed.

"So?" said Larry. "This guy's been going on and on about you all week long. Your long, silky black hair, your dark brown eyes like infinite pools of blah blah blah. Oh, and the cute little freckles around your nose, and then something about the little dimple above your upper lip."

"He brought my philtrum into this? Wow."

"There's a word for that thing?" Larry asked. "See, you two little lovenerds are perfect for each other! Oh and of course he had plenty to say about your brain and your personality and all that, but if I'm being honest I was tuning most of it out by then. Anyway, my point is, he won't shut up. It's a little embarrassing. So, like, do you want to go on a date with him, or what?"

"I don't know, maybe. He seems nice enough. What about you, what's your situation?"

"Oh. Me?" Larry asked. "I'm kind of...married to my work."

"What work?" Randy grumbled.

"Just trying to help you out here, buddy," replied Larry.

"You know he's a registered Republican?" Randy asked. "I mean he probably voted for—"

"He Who Shall Not Be Named," Larry interrupted. "And I didn't, but—"

"Ah, right," laughed Randy. "As we both already know, Roommate Rule #3 clearly states that we do not discuss He Who Shall Not Be Named, She Who Also Shall Not Be Named, or Shia LaBeouf."

"Why Shia LaBeouf?" asked Kelli.

"He just really upsets us both," said Randy.

"Huh. Ok," Kelli sighed. "But I mean, you've seen Larry, right? He's tall, and handsome, and pretty ripped..."

"I know," said Randy, "Trust me, as a pansexual, I'm well aware. He's like a big, dumb, glorious Statue of David."

"I'm right here, you guys," said Larry.

"Hey, we're just stating the obvious," Kelli replied. "That's the assignment, right? Now Randy, what exactly is a pansexual? Like, you get turned on by bread or something?"

"I thought you were an omnisexual," added Larry.

"It's the same thing! I think. It just means that I'm open to natural, consensual experiences with all kinds of individuals..."

"Even though he's literally only ever been with girls," Larry said.

"Women!" said Randy, perhaps a bit louder than he'd intended. "Er, sorry. And I said I was *open*."

"I was just messing with you," said Kelli. "I knew what it was. But you know, you're kind of cute when you get flustered. Anyway, why are you asking me, Larry? Randy's right here. He can ask me himself."

"Oh, I just knew he was never going to get around to it," said Larry. "He's a bit shy. Also he basically thinks anything a man says to a woman is a form of sexual aggression."

"Not *anything*," muttered Randy. "Just, you know. Most things. Anyway, I hardly think Kelli needs you to mansplain sexual aggression to her."

Kelli just looked at him, one eyebrow slightly raised.

"Oh, sorry," said Randy, "See, mansplaining is when—"

Her raised right forefinger stopped him short. "Tell me you are *not* about to mansplain mansplaining to me!"

Randy's cheeks reddened. Larry laughed.

"So where are you from, anyway?" Larry asked Kelli. "Are you, like, Middle-Eastern, or Asian or something like that?"

"Something like that," Kelli replied.

"Whaaat?" Larry asked defensively, noticing that Randy's

cranium looked dangerously close to self-destructing. "People can be from places. Jesus."

"Time's up," announced Judy, who rather vocally preferred that her students just call her Judy. "I hope you had fun practicing your forced exposition. Next week we're on to mixed metaphors. Be sure to do the reading, or you may find yourselves up shit creek without a parachute!"

Randy and Kelli chortled.

"I'm so lost," said Larry.

"Well, I'll see you guys next week, then," said Kelli.

"Right," said Randy. "Next week. Oh, hey, I may not be here, though. There's a work thing. My boss says he's got some kind of project for me, which usually means a lot of overtime."

"Oh?" she asked. "What do you do?"

"I'm an I.T. Guy," he answered. "You know. Saving the world, one minor technical annoyance at a time."

"Cool," Kelli smiled. "Well, if I don't see you next week, good luck saving the world!"

2. CALL ME MABY

"You know I'm going to murder you in your sleep one of these days," Randy said, as they exited the building onto 54th Street.

"I know," Larry replied.

"Good. Drink?"

"Drink."

"I'll have a gin martini, please. Something complex, with herbal or floral notes preferably, and your driest vermouth, gently mingled."

"Yes, Sir," said the bartender, offering his finest Botox-straining smile. His playful polka-dot bowtie and suspenders and painstakingly sculpted faux hawk suggested that most of his tips went into headshots. "And for you?"

"A beer, please," responded Larry.

"And what kind of beer would you like, Sir?"

"Your nearest."

"Sir, we have over a hundred and twenty beers from around the world, I would be happy to show you—"

"Look, buddy," said Larry, "my friend just ordered like a pregnant yoga instructor at a Starbucks, and you didn't bat an eye. I would like a beer, please. If that causes you anxiety, you can take it up with your therapist at your next session. Where I come from, a beer is a beer."

"Then perhaps you'd be happier if you went back there."

"Well now, that seems a bit racist."

"Sir, we're both clearly white."

"Well, it's something-ist."

"We need a wall," said Larry, sipping his beer.

"I cannot even believe you Conservatives," Randy said. "For the last time, we do not need your ludicrous wall! There's security in place already. It's a fake problem. What good will it even do?"

"What security?" Larry laughed. "And why even bring politics into this? It's completely open. Anybody can just waltz in and act like they own the place. Hey, you want to get a bunch of stuff for free? We don't have any wall, come on over here and take anything you want for free!"

"Seriously?" said Randy. "You know they can't just get things for free."

"Then why did I find Mr. Krishnamurti's cat eating my Lucky Charms this morning?"

"Why did you—? Wait, what are you—? Ohhhhh..." said Randy. "Right. The landlord said he was going to fix that wall like three weeks ago."

"Uh huh."

"We need a wall," said Randy, sipping his martini.

"I'm so sick of Craig Kim," said Randy.

"Who?" Larry asked.

"You know, the guy who—"

"—you literally never shut up about?" Larry interrupted. "Yeah, no, now I remember. Go on."

"I mean, I meet the guy at one of those alumni events and he keeps saying he remembers me from school, and then he wants a referral because we have some open position in Sales at work, like I know the first thing about those cretins in Sales..."

"Uh huh," said Larry, looking down at his phone.

"...so I basically get him this job, and now he can't stop coming around punching me on the arm like 'Rand-AY!' and talking in his stupid Sales brospeak and then asking me for favors."

Larry glanced up from his phone. "Like, sexual?"

"No! Why would you—No, man, just work stuff! Help with his projects and stuff like that."

"Ah," said Larry, his gaze redescending.

"So?" asked Randy. "What do you think I should do about this guy?"

"You could have him murdered," suggested Larry, without looking up.

"What?"

"I don't know, dude, this all sounds like pretty normal job stuff. That's why I generally try to avoid having one. I find them highly overrated. Need another drink?"

"Uh huh."

"'See you guys next week,' she says," muttered Randy, taking a sip of his martini that evolved into more of a gulp. He looked around at the bar decor, which suddenly seemed far too bright and far too modern to properly facilitate his ill humor.

"Ah, guess we'll be talking about this, then," said Larry.

"'You guys.' Not me, mind you. Just us guys as a collective whole. At the normal allotted time next week and not one second sooner." Randy sighed. "Oh well. C'est la vie. But I mean, seriously, how beautiful is this girl?"

"Uh, sorry but I've been told they're called *women*," laughed Larry. "Yeah, she's pretty cute I guess."

"Cute?" Randy looked at him incredulously. "Cute? No, no. Helen of Troy was cute..."

"What? When did Troy even have a girlfriend? I swear nobody ever tells me anything around here!"

Randy's jaw dropped slightly. "How do you remember to breathe?" he asked.

"What? Seriously, I'm so lost."

"And her mind!" Randy continued. "Like, did you hear that thing she said about Schopenhauer in class today?"

"Yeah, I didn't get that at all," Larry said.

"Yeah, no, me neither," Randy said. "But it sounded totally insightful and relevant. Had I, you know. Understood it."

"Probably," said Larry. "Oh, hey, speaking of women, guess who I've been seeing through SugarMaby."

"Good gods," Randy said. "You're still doing that sugar baby thing?"

"It's 'Maby,' like a male baby. And like hey, is this whole thing kind of awkward? I don't know, maybe. You'd be surprised, there are a lot of very bored women out there with too much money."

"*You* have too much money!"

"That's my parents' money. It's nice to feel a bit more self-sufficient sometimes."

"By preying on lonely older women?" Randy nodded with mock approval.

"Right. So guess who I've been seeing."

"Who?"

"Delphine."

"Who?"

"Delphine. You know, that nice lady we were talking to at your Christmas party."

Randy's eyes widened. "Delphine, my boss's wife, Delphine?"

"Uhm... could be?"

"Oh, no, she definitely is! And this seemed like a good idea to you?"

"I don't know."

Randy rubbed his eyes nervously. "So like...are you..."

"What? No! I mean, she's not that bad-looking though, right? But no, nothing like that. She's just really bored, you know? I mean her husband—"

"Frank, my boss," interrupted Randy. "The large, angry man who employs me."

"Yeah, that one," Larry continued. "He's never around, and she wants to do things. You know, she's really into animals? She took me to the aquarium the other day."

"Well, that sounds sweet," said Randy. "Now if you'll excuse me, I think I have to go throw up and then update my resume."

"Oh, ok. Hey, can I finish your drink? This beer is terrible."

3. IN AGREEMENT

The following morning, like most mornings, Randy took the 7 and N trains to 23rd St., crossed Madison Square Park on foot, greeted the doorman at his office building on Park Avenue South, and hit the elevator button marked "HERC Data Technologies."

"Good morning, Randy," said Doris, the Executive Admin, seated at the reception desk. She looked to be about seventy, with curly white hair and little reading glasses. "Gingerdoodle?"

"Sorry?"

Doris held up a plate of cookies. "Gingerdoodles. They're like snickerdoodles and ginger snaps combined."

"Cool, thanks," said Randy, taking one. "Hey, did Frank happen to say anything about— *Oh my gods*, this is delicious! What is in this cookie? Doris, I think this may be the best thing that's ever been in my mouth. Sorry, I'm gonna need another one of these. Thanks. Now…what were we talking about?"

"Frank," said Doris. "Yes, he was looking for you. Catch him now, he's got a 9:03."

"A 9:0—Uh…Ok, thanks."

"Hey, guys," he said to no one in particular, as he hurried down the cubicle aisle on the way to Frank's office. He passed through the Marketing department, then into Sales, when—

"POW! Rand-AY!" came a familiar voice, along with a familiar rush of pain in his upper arm.

It was Craig Kim.

"I'm in a bit of a hurry right now, Craig Kim," Randy said.

"Oh I feel you, Randy! Work hard, play hard, am I right? Fist bump!"

Randy pushed his crumpled hand awkwardly into Craig Kim's.

"Oh so uh, Randster," continued Craig Kim. "I need a little teeny tiny favor."

"Shocking," said Randy. "Look, I'm—"

"So I'm at a sales call with a client, you know."

"No, not really."

"And she says to me Craig Kim, I need you to synergize my backend. And I'm all like DAMN, baby, I'll synergize the hell out of that backend!"

"Charming," said Randy.

"But then she's all no, silly, I mean our I.T. backend! And then I totally banged her, obviously, but I'm going to need you to take care of that other thing she was talking about."

"With the synergizing?" Randy asked. "See, that's pretty vague, and—"

"Well look, Bro, I think what she's getting at is that you need to take her I.T. backend, and like...synergize it more. Like a lot."

"Right," said Randy. "The thing is, though, is that I hear you saying words, Craig Kim, but those words don't seem to have any actual meaning. Also I really just handle our corporate I.T., not the cli—"

"Sweet! I knew you'd be all over this. So like, when can we launch?"

"Uh..." Randy shook his head, trying to think clearly. "How about lunch?"

"We can launch at lunch?"

"No," said Randy. "How about you buy me lunch and try to explain a bit—"

"Rand-AY, my man! Protip, Bro, I only do lunch with clients! Time is money and money is...money, am I right? Alright, ball's in your court Randy, let's get this ship rolling. Glad we could have this talk!"

Craig Kim carried on steamrolling his way down the cubicle aisle, leaving Randy staring after him with a blank expression.

"I'm so sick of Craig Kim," Randy muttered to himself, then continued toward Frank's office.

Randy found Frank's office door open as usual, with Frank sitting behind his sprawling mahogany desk, his hulking frame squeezed into his executive swively chair, feet up, barking into his wired landline phone.

"No, no, look. I don't care about the fucking user agreement!" Frank was shouting. He gave Randy a grin and a wink and gestured to the ordinary, somewhat short, decidedly non-swively chair in front of his desk. Randy sat.

"Come on, Lucian," Frank continued. "Lucian. Lucian! Listen for a second. Enough with this shit about your agreement. I didn't read the agreement. Do you read user agreements? No, fuck off, you do not. Look, my tech guys talked to your yes guys, and your yes guys told them yes, and we bought your platform. That's how business works, Lucian. So go tell your tech guys to make the ones and zeroes do whatever the hell they're not doing, so I can have my fucking morning cup of coffee in peace for once in my life!" There was a short, uncomfortable pause. "Yeah? Perfect. Now, I have to go. Someone's in my office." He paused. "What? What do you care? It's the Queen of England, Lucian. She looks pissed. Gotta go." He hung up the phone.

"We should probably start reading user agreements," Frank said. "Hey, Randy. Let's see, Randy. Randy, Randy, Randy. Uhm… Oh! Right. Server upgrades. So that got approved. That means live updates in person at the main offices in London, Tokyo, and Geneva in the extremely near future. You in?"

"Uh...sure."

"Sweet! Boys' trip! Oh, I'll be going too, see, I have other business. Sales-team pow-wow across the sites, you know. Now,

Doris will set everything up. Crap, I hope my wife doesn't insist on going. She probably will. Or maybe not, I think she might be seeing somebody. Oh! That reminds me, short-notice travel means you can bring a companion and corporate will pay for everything."

"Oh," said Randy. "I don't really have—"

"Doesn't matter!" interrupted Frank. "Bring whoever. New corporate policy is no questions asked. Too many hassles in the past trying to play Who's Who, now it's basically just anybody with a pulse. You must have some girl, or guy... I mean I know you're... you know. Whatever you are. It's cool. Hey, bring that dude from the Christmas party! He was a hoot."

"Oh, he really is," said Randy. "You have no idea."

"Awesome," Frank grinned. "So you'll bring him?"

"Uh... Maybe?"

4. PLAN B

"He wants you to travel around the world, to upgrade some server software?" Larry asked, raising an eyebrow.

"Yep," Randy replied.

They were in their messy, cramped apartment in Queens, sitting on the cracked green leather couch that they'd recently dragged in off the street to replace the empty space where a couch should be.

"But couldn't you, like, upgrade the software from here? I thought that's how computers work."

"Yeah, probably."

"So did you—"

"It didn't really come up," grinned Randy. "But, get this. He says the company will pay for me to bring somebody with me. Just, like, anybody I want. So I was thinking—"

"Dude," said Larry, "You have to ask Kelli!"

"Kelli, like the girl who didn't say yes to a date, Kelli?"

"*Woman*," said Larry. "And yes, that one. Sure, she didn't say yes right away to a *regular* date with you, but let's be real. What do you even do on a first date? I'm thinking organic coffee, probably in some loud, overcrowded hipster place with unfinished wooden tables, surrounded by self-employed writers and graphic designers who live out of their cars somewhere in Brooklyn and don't shower as often as they should. So let's call that Plan A. And then along comes Plan B, a free trip around the world. I mean, I gotta think she may have a different opinion about Plan B. Think about it, what's more romantic than asking a girl...er, a *woman*, to see the world with you?"

"Romantic, psychotic…"

"'Scuse me," Larry said, pulling his phone out of the pocket of his tacky track pants and starting to dial. "I forgot I was supposed to make a call."

"Who are you—?"

"Oh, hey Kell, it's Larry."

"Please," laughed Randy. "You don't even know her number."

"Randy's friend Larry," Larry continued. "From writing class? Right, exactly. We did that exercise together where we had to have awkward conversations and say things we all knew already, in order to practice one of the elements of bad writing or something. Right. Our teacher Judy thinks that it will help us improve our natural style. No, yeah, I know, I just wanted to try it out one more time. You know I think I'm finally starting to get the hang of it! What's that? Yeah, I know, right? This conversation is definitely kind of awkward."

Larry gave Randy a wink.

"Who are you even talking to?" Randy asked. "Your mom? HI LARRY'S MOM!"

"Yeah, that was Randy. He doesn't think I have your number. Anyway, listen. Randy has to take a work trip around the world and he gets to bring somebody, all expenses paid. Oh, uh… London, Taiwan, I think, and…some Scandinavian place or something. So what do you think, do you want to go with him?"

He turned to Randy and put his hand over his phone. "She said that sounds really weird."

"That's what I said!" shouted Randy.

"Yeah, that's what he said, too," Larry said to whoever was, in fact, on the other end. "Alright, maybe that was a crazy idea. My bad. Hey, how about when he gets back from seeing the wonders of the world all by his lonesome self, you let him take you out for a coffee? I mean, the guy is nuts about you. Uh huh? Ok. Cool, see you in class. Buh-bye."

Randy glared at Larry.

"What?" asked Larry.

"What the hell was that about?!"

"Think about it," Larry grinned. "Five minutes ago, going on a date with you, or Plan A as I like to call it, probably sounded like a big deal. Now it sounds like a really, really normal thing to do."

"Wait," said Randy. "Are you talking about extremeness aversion bias?"

"Uh...that depends," Larry replied with a puzzled expression. "Is your thing you just said like the thing that I just said?"

"Yes."

"Then yes," confirmed Larry in a confident tone.

"Oh, don't try to give me a lecture on semantics," Randy sighed.

"I didn't even know that's something I could do!" said Larry. "That's going right on my resume. How do you spell that?"

"You have a resume?"

"I could have a resume."

"Whatever," said Randy. "So...she said yes?"

"She said she'd think about it."

5. LOST IN TRANSLATION

"God, I hate Soho," grumbled Larry.

"Everybody hates Soho," Randy replied, as they wriggled their way around hordes of chattering, heavily perfumed window-gawking tourists dressed like designer circus extras.

"Alright," said Larry, "Here's Houston street."

"HOW-ston," Randy corrected.

"What?"

"It's pronounced HOW-ston."

"No. That's ridiculous," said Larry. "Just nope. Now where is this place?"

"Let's see," Randy said, looking into his phone, "it should be somewhere... over... there. Holy crap, look at that line!"

"Jesus. There's a line around the block. Are you sure that's not the cronut place?"

"Nah, that's down a few blocks," said Randy.

"Like, south?"

"New Yorkers say 'downtown,' or just 'down,'" Randy replied.

"Humans say 'south.' Or just 'that way over there.'"

"Well, regardless, this is the place," said Randy. "And with a line like that, we're definitely not making it to writing class afterwards. Which sucks, because I was really hoping to see Kelli one more time before the trip. You know, this is all your fault! What kind of grown man doesn't have a passport?"

"What kind of grown man knows where the cronut place is?"

"Hey. Cronuts are delightful!"

"Damn it," Larry said, "you're right, they're pretty amazing. I'm sorry, I'm just tired and a little hungry. Anyway, what's the big deal? I don't see why anyone would even want to leave America."

"You're an idiot. Are you telling me you wouldn't want to see the pyramids? Or the Taj Mahal? Or the canals of Venice?"

"I have a TV," said Larry. "Now, let's go wait in line."

"Wait ON line," said Randy. "Seriously, how long have you lived in New York?"

"Longer than you have," replied Larry. "I just have a lower tolerance for bullshit."

"How much longer do you think this'll take?" Larry muttered. "We've moved like ten feet and I swear this little ginger baby in front of us has grown about two inches since we got in this line."

"You'll have to excuse him," Randy said to the couple standing in line just ahead of them, the mother rocking a small baby in her arms. "He gets a little cranky when he hasn't had a nap. And may I say, that's a beautiful baby you have. How old is she?"

"Five months, yesterday," the father said proudly. "She's our pride and joy. And now we're getting ready to go to her auntie's wedding in Wales, so she's getting her first passport!"

"Oh, well that's just adorable," Randy said. He looked at Larry. "Hey, my little guy here is getting his first passport too."

"Huh. How old is he?" asked the father.

"I'm not really sure, actually," said Randy. "Thirty...something."

"Well, you must be very proud too," said the mother, looking Larry up and down just a little more than was strictly necessary. "He's a handsome one."

"Er...thanks," said Randy. "People keep telling me that."

6. THE FRIENDLY SKIES

"What?" asked Larry.

"What, what?" replied Randy.

"You're giving me that look again. So, spit it out."

"Well," said Randy. "Don't you think you're being a bit of an asshole?"

"I mean, I didn't, since I'm literally just sitting here doing nothing. But clearly you're going to enlighten me."

"Look around you," Randy said, indicating the surrounding passengers in the United Boeing 777. "Nobody has their seat leaned back except you."

"Huh," said Larry. "Welp. Guess I'm the Alpha. Go, me. Now if you'll excuse me, I'm going to have a nap."

"It's the guy behind you who you should be asking to excuse you."

"Never met him. And he's got his own button to recline himself, if he doesn't like it."

"Haven't you ever heard of a social contract?" asked Randy.

"What, like on Facebook? Nobody reads the user agreements, Randy," laughed Larry. "And I'm sorry, but they shouldn't give me a button if they don't want me to push it. I'm not some kind of lab rat."

"You've got the manners of one," Randy said.

"Hardly," said Larry. "I read that rats are actually very car-ing and sensitive creatures. Much like you. That's why they live in cages and sewers."

"Wait, you read something?" asked Randy.

"Don't you know they proved that being selfish leads to the best outcomes for everyone? It's a known fact."

"According to who?"

"I don't know," Larry said. "Ayn Rand, or Michael Douglas or somebody. Greed is good, Randy. Look it up."

"Whatever," said Randy. "I hope you're comfortable in your reclined seat. You're basically a terrorist."

"Excuse me," said a voice from behind Larry, in a very sophisticated British accent. "Would you please mind your language? My son has a recital and I'd like to get there rather than have our flight grounded, if it's all the same to you."

"Sorry, Sir," Larry said, looking directly at Randy rather than turning around. "My friend has poor social skills. Is he making you uncomfortable?"

"A bit, yes," said the man.

"Randy," said Larry, "you're making the gentleman behind me uncomfortable."

"You know what?" Randy said. "You can both fuck off."

"Sir," said a flight attendant, striding up the aisle from behind them, "I'm going to have to ask you to put your seatback up for takeoff."

"Certainly," Larry said, smiling up at the young woman. "And may I just say, you have lovely eyes."

"Oh!" she said, blushing visibly. "Uh...well, thank you." She hurried forward and continued with her duties, though not without glancing back once or twice in the process.

"I don't mind the rest, either," Larry said, leaning a bit to see better as she moved further up the aisle.

"You're still gonna have to put your seat up, you know," Randy grumbled.

"I'll get to it."

"I have a feeling this is gonna be a long flight," said Randy.

"Amen," muttered the man seated behind Larry.

"POP! Rand-AY!" cried Craig Kim, hitting Randy on the shoulder as they passed each other in the aisle. "We're on the same plane, Broseph! What are the odds, right?"

"Well, Doris booked us all, so..."

"Ha! Love that old broad! I bet she was hella fine, back in the day. I mean way, way, back in the day, right? So, what're you doing, man? Off to take a fat dump?"

"No, Craig Kim," said Randy. "Who even does that on an airplane?"

"Uh...certainly no one I know!" said Craig Kim with an enthusiastic laugh. "But maybe don't go in the second bathroom on the left for a while, if you catch my drift."

Randy sniffed. "I think I do a little, now that you mention it."

"Ha! Classic! Say, Randy, how is that synergizing project going?"

"I mean, I would say it's less of a project and more of a random assortment of vague buzzwords haphazardly slapped together."

"Right," said Craig Kim. "But, like, if you were to quantify, how synergized would you say we are at this point?"

Randy stared at Craig Kim, wondering if he was really as oblivious as he seemed. "We're 52.7% synergized," he said finally.

Craig Kim nodded. "Not bad," he said. "But we're gonna need it higher than that. I'll keep checking in."

"*God, I hate that Craig Kim,*" he muttered to himself as he continued down the aisle.

◆ ◆ ◆

"So...what does your company do?" asked Larry.

"Big Data," said Randy.

"Ah," said Larry. "Right. So...what does your company do?"

"It's a long story," said Randy.

Larry looked out the window next to Randy, where there was nothing but endless gray-green ocean waves as far as the eye could see. Next he glanced around the airplane cabin, where everyone was either asleep or engaged in a movie on their personal screens. "I think we're good," he said.

"Well, we design web services and APIs as well as end-user solutions for massive-scale data processing," Randy said.

"Huh. And what's that used for?"

"I don't know," Randy said. "I'm just the I.T. guy. I work on the computers. That's client business, and the Accounts teams deal with it. You know, the clients just do...Big Data stuff."

"So basically you're spies," Larry said.

"What?"

"Clearly your company is part of a Deep State government conspiracy," Larry said. "And they must be planning something important, sending you around the world for this server upgrade. You're Big Brother!"

Randy paused, staring at Larry with increasingly wide eyes.

"Nuh-uh," he said.

7. LONDON TOWN

"Welcome to London," Randy said, looking around at the Heathrow airport terminal full of shiny shops and restaurants. "How does it feel to be out of America for the first time?"

"I should've brought my guns," Larry replied.

"You can't bring guns here," Randy laughed. "And anyway, you don't even have guns."

"Oh, I have guns. In America. I just don't have guns in New York City, because New York City isn't America. Plus I'd have nowhere to put them, anyway. You should see my gun storage room back home, it's bigger than our apartment."

"Are you—? Do you really—?" Randy stuttered. "Wait, what the hell do you have all those guns for?"

"You know," said Larry, nonchalantly. "Terrorists, the government…"

"So your imaginary enemies are the people who want to take down America…and America?"

"Hey, laugh it up now, but when the inevitable breakdown of civilization comes, you'll see. It's better to have it and need it…wait, no. It's better to need it and…and… Look, it's just better to have it! But of course the Commies running New York don't really see it that way."

"So why'd you move to New York, then?" asked Randy.

"Because, do you have any idea how boring America is?" Larry laughed.

"You mean just…other than the constant threat of government invasion and zombie apocalypse scenarios?"

"Right," said Larry.

"Oooookay," replied Randy. "Huh. So it says here we just need to take the Heathrow Express to Paddington."

"To Paddington?"

"Yes."

"The cartoon bear?"

"It's the name of a train station," said Randy.

"They named a train station after a cartoon bear? Jesus. I guess I really didn't need the guns after all."

"Well," said Randy, as they stepped off the train. "We are officially in London Town. I don't have to report in to the office until tomorrow morning, and Frank had other business. What should we do?"

The two of them paused, glancing around the platform at Paddington Station, for a good several minutes.

"Drink?" asked Larry.

"Drink," said Randy.

They walked into the old pub and looked around in awe at the intricate woodwork, antique bar fixtures, and Victorian decor. The place was fairly empty, with a smattering of tourists having a break from their afternoon sightseeing activities, and a few grizzled old-timers who seemed to be installed permanently as part of the ambience.

"Hi," said Larry to nobody in particular. "We're Randy and Larry."

"Nope," said the bartender, coming around from behind the bar. "Not in my fookin' pub yer not!"

"Was that weird?" asked Randy, still sitting on the cobblestone walkway outside of the pub.

"I've never been out of America," Larry said, "but that did seem weird. I think that's the first time I've been literally thrown out of a bar."

"That man was inhumanly strong. My ass hurts. Does your ass hurt?"

"Yeah, a little. People are mean here."

"Well," said Randy, getting up slowly. "What do you want to do now?"

"Definitely not have a drink," replied Larry, who remained seated. "Hey, you wanna check out the Eiffel Tower?"

Randy just stared at him, mouth slightly agape, looking for any hint of a smile.

"No," he said finally, in the most condescending tone he could presently muster, from among his broad spectrum of condescending tones, whilst brushing gravel from his ass.

"Fine, then what do you suggest?" asked Larry.

"We could go see Big Ben."

"Randy, I thought I'd made it clear that I'm not into the gay stuff."

Randy was about to respond when he suddenly became aware of a presence some yards away from them. He looked up, and saw an elderly man dressed in tattered corduroy pants, an old plaid shirt, and a woolen vest. His face was gaunt and clean-shaven and his head bald, and he stood staring at them through big bulging eyes that sat unblinking beneath scraggly, unkempt gray eyebrows.

"Larry," Randy whispered. "Don't look, but there's a really creepy old man staring at us."

"Huh," said Larry in his regular tone of voice. As Randy knew well by now, Larry really only had one volume. "What does he look like?"

"Like a creepy old man!" Randy whisper-yelled.

"Sure, but like… 53-year-old guy with a greased toupee in a convertible Mustang leering at your teenage daughter creepy? Or like Garfield Halloween Special old man creepy?"

"The Garfield one!" whispered Randy. "Shit, he's coming

toward us."

The old man wobbled toward them.

Time passed.

"Is he getting here, or what?" asked Larry.

"Well, he's really creepy but he's also extremely slow," whispered Randy.

Larry turned to look. "Hey, guy," he called out, picking himself up off the ground while dusting off his pants. "You were in the bar back there."

"I know who you are," said the old man in a deep, gravelly voice with a heavy British accent.

"Well, we did kind of announce it," said Larry. "I'm Larry. He's Randy. We're—"

"You are the one," the old man interrupted.

"The what, now?" asked Randy. "Which one? I mean, which of us is what one?"

"The One," repeated the man, this time in carefully enunciated capital letters.

"We're two," offered Larry. "He's one, and I'm another one. So...two."

"It is the fulfillment of the prophecies that have been given unto us. The day of reckoning approaches! The time is nigh!"

"The time is...?" asked Larry.

"Nigh!" repeated the old man dramatically.

"I'm sorry, what's 'nigh'?" asked Larry.

"It means near," whispered Randy.

"Then why doesn't he just say near?"

"I don't know!" Randy whisper-shouted. "He's old and creepy and British! And why am I still whispering when he can clearly hear me from right there?!"

The old man didn't seem to notice their side chatter. "Heed my words," he continued. "You must proceed with great caution. Those who appear to be your friends will prove to be your enemies. And those who are your enemies will become your allies. Beware of false idols! You must face your greatest weakness, and make it your strength in the final hour when all seems lost. Remember in their entirety these words, if you wish to attain the ultimate goal."

"Uhhh...k," said Larry. "So all the things are the opposite things. Got it."

"Is there, like, a hidden camera around here?" Randy asked, looking around at the old stone walls of the bar and the neighboring buildings.

"I would say this guy's been reading too much Young Adult Fiction," added Larry, "but..." he gesticulated toward the old man.

The old man turned, slowly, and began walking back toward the bar.

"Hey, Wise Old Man!" called Randy. "Don't we get, like, a magic sword or anything?"

"A sack of beans?" suggested Larry.

"Invisibility cloak?" Randy added.

The old man ignored them, and continued to maneuver toward the bar at a glacial pace. A minute or two passed.

"Hey, guy," called Larry. "Why did your friend throw us out of the bar, anyway?"

Finally the old man turned slowly to look back at them.

"Welcome to Jolly Old England," he said, and spat on the ground. "Your friend's name means horny. And yours means rowdy and shitfaced."

"Huh," said Larry. "Well that's something."

"So we just walked into a bar and announced that we were drunk, horny, and looking for trouble," said Randy.

"Yeah, that response actually seems kind of fair now," agreed Larry.

"I feel like that's the only useful thing that creepy old man said to us in his entire ominous monologue," said Randy. "And now, I think I do want to find that drink."

"Hey, maybe there's another less weird bar nigh," suggested Larry.

"Another less weird bar what, now?"

"Nigh," said Larry, reading the look on Randy's face. "No?"

"No."

8. UPON WESTMINSTER BRIDGE

"And that's it?" asked Delphine. "Just a lot of silliness about friends becoming enemies, and dogs and cats living together, and things being nigh? It all seems quite vague and unactionable."

"Right?" agreed Larry.

"Let's forget about all of that, and just enjoy the fact that we're here in London, our men are off working, it's a beautiful afternoon, and we haven't a care in the world!"

"You're not going to let that go, about me being Randy's plus one for the trip," said Larry.

"Not for a single moment!" laughed Delphine.

They were having a stroll along Westminster Bridge overlooking the Thames, and Larry couldn't help but notice that with the cool breeze lightly caressing her tastefully coiffed short hair, which was jet black streaked with touches of gray that bespoke sophistication and hard-earned life experience, sending the odd strand momentarily pirouetting across her angular yet playful features, and with her slender, graceful figure accentuated by an elegant floral sundress well suited to the preternatural warmth of the early spring day, her appearance was quite striking not only for a woman of her age, but indeed for a woman of any age.

"You look good," Larry said.

"Thank you, you're sweet," Delphine replied. She had just a touch of some accent that Larry couldn't quite identify. Which, as Randy would have pointed out, effectively narrowed it down to all of the accents.

Randy, who, for some reason, had been trying to call him roughly every two minutes for quite some time now.

"Do you need to take that?" asked Delphine, as his phone continued vibrating and hurling robotic bleeps and bloops in his general direction.

"No, sorry," Larry said. "I'm sure it's nothing. We got these local burner phones for the trip, and I haven't figured out how to shut it up." He looked down at the river below. "Hey, do you think you could swim in this thing?"

"Oh," laughed Delphine, "you wouldn't imagine all of the wondrous creatures that do! You know, about fifty years ago, that water was so polluted that it was declared biologically dead. Too many decades of Dickensian industrialization, you know."

"Oh, yeah, totally," said Larry. "All of that...thing you just said."

"But look at it now," she continued. "They say it's one of the cleanest rivers in the world, and whole aquatic ecosystems have begun to flourish again. You can find all kinds of fish, eels, seahorses, seals. Even the occasional dolphin!"

"Huh," said Larry. He glanced at his phone and saw *Pick up your ducking phone. *ducking. Ducking autocorrect!*

"Hey," he went on. "So do you know what this whole trip thing is about, with the server upgrades and all? It just seems like with—"

"Darling!" Delphine chided, "you know I detest shop talk. If I wanted to know about business I could spend time with my exasperating boor of a husband. There are far more pressing matters in the world, you know. For instance, I need shoes."

"Shoes?"

"Shoes. The per diem on this corporate card isn't just

going to misappropriate itself. So, are you in?"

"I have no idea what you just said, but sure." said Larry. "I guess I could use shoes. Oh, hey. That rhymes!"

"It certainly does," laughed Delphine. "Now come along, I know just the place for a couple of gals like us to treat our feet."

9. THE OFFICE (UK)

"Greetings, everyone!" said Simon Worthington III, head of the London office, who had called all of the employees together in the break room. He was dressed in a light gray tailored three-piece suit with a lavender tie, and had the dashing good looks of someone who might be chosen to play the next James Bond. "Allow me to introduce Randy. You are to assist him in any way he deems necessary. Randy is the one who has been sent unto us. Er...you know. From the New York office. For the server thing."

"Nice to meet you all," Randy added with a wave and a slight nod. "I'm just the I.T. Guy. Just here to, uh, update the servers. No biggie."

He was looking around at his assembled colleagues, including Frank, Craig Kim, and several others from his office, when his eyes happened upon a stunning redhead wearing a form-fitting electric blue dress, and refused to move any further. She caught him staring and offered him a sly grin in response.

"The modesty of a true gentleman!" said Simon. "But let there be no mistake—Randy is the representative who was chosen by our human leaders. For the computer thing. Now, off to the races with you all. And for those attending the Sales meetings, we'll assemble in Conference Room C in ten minutes. Cheerio!"

"Thank you for that introduction," Randy said to Simon as the crowd began to disperse. "It was very..."

"Conspicuous, yes," said Simon. "Well, we must make sure

everyone knows exactly who you are."

"Yeah, cool," said Randy, feeling slightly uneasy. Why did Simon find it necessary to introduce the I.T. Guy, and not anyone else from the New York and other offices? Had they all visited previously? "So, uh, the servers are in that back room over there?"

"Yes," Simon replied. "You should be able to access everything you need with your card dealie and your pass code thing."

"Great. I'm going to set up a test build back there, and then I'll need to use somebody's computer to access it and run some test scripts and such. That part may take an hour or so."

"Certainly," Simon said. "I have a business lunch with an associate near Leicester Square, so you're welcome to have my computer for your testing. My assistant Octavia will show you into my office when you're ready. You'll find her just over there, along the wall aisle outside my office. She's the redhead in the blue dress. If you're a heterosexual you'll have noticed her already. Oh, and ask her for the memory whatsit I've left for you. Cheerio!"

Randy grinned and headed back toward the server room, whistling quietly to himself as he walked.

"Hello, Octavia? I'm—"

"Randy," she said with a smile, looking up at him from her desk.

"Very," he mumbled dreamily. "Er, very pleased to meet you, that is."

"The pleasure," she said, "is all mine. Speaking of which, have you any plans for dinner this evening? London can be a confusing town, and I know a nice little place..."

"That sounds lovely," Randy sighed, "but unfortunately not possible. I'm running a limited test upgrade on the servers now, but I have to roll out the real version this evening after everyone's gone home. Even with no issues it'll take me well into the night."

"I'm sorry to hear that," Octavia said with an exaggerated pout. "And tomorrow?"

"Assuming all goes well, my flight's in the morning."

"Well, a girl can try," she laughed. "Another time, then. Simon's office is open. Password on the computer is GoHumansGo1234, upper camel case."

"Odd choice," Randy mused. "Oh, did Simon leave some sort of memory device for me? Maybe a flash drive or something?"

"Right," Octavia said hesitantly. "Yes, well. Simon did give me this flash drive."

"Great. What's on it?"

"I'm afraid I don't know," Octavia replied. "Something he thought you'd be needing for your...assignment, no doubt. By the way, they've got you going to the Tokyo office tomorrow, and then to Geneva on Tuesday morning, is it?"

"Yes," Randy confirmed. "Why?"

"Interesting," she said with a distant air. "Oh, no reason. Only that I shall have to make sure my...colleagues are adequately prepared for your arrival."

"Uhm...cool. Thank you."

"The pleasure is all mine," she said.

"Yes, you've said. I'll just, uh..." he finger-jabbed a few times in the direction of Simon's office.

"Certainly."

Randy quickly snatched the flash drive from her extended hand and backed his way into the office, closing the door behind him on impulse.

"That was a strange conversation," he said to himself. "Now," he continued, looking at the flash drive. "What is on you?"

He logged into Simon's computer without trouble, and went to insert the flash drive into the nearest slot, but then he hesitated. He knew very well that putting unknown flash drives into unknown computers was asking for trouble.

"Ah well," he said to himself. "His flash drive, his computer. I'll trust he knows what he's doing."

He pushed the drive in, and waited. A few seconds later, a window popped up. It was a simple gray-and-black job with one line of text: *ARE YOU A REAL HUMAN?*, followed by two buttons marked *YES* and *NO*.

"Of course I'm a human," Randy said to himself. "Guess it's just some kind of CAPTCHA protocol. But then again…"

Randy continued staring at the screen. "Am I a real human?" he asked nobody in particular. Nobody in particular failed to respond.

"Descartes would say that I think I'm human, therefore I am human. After all, thinking is both the hallmark and the unique prerogative of the human species. On the other hand, Eastern philosophies would posit that I have no fixed and unchanging nature that might be termed 'human,' but that my human-ness is evolving at every moment in a web of interconnected subrealities that defies such simple definition. Unless, of course, one takes the word itself to imply the amorphous end product of such a complex system, thus embracing the paradox of the absolute versus relative definitions of reality contained within the verb 'to be' itself, as viewed through a dharmic paradigm…"

"*Everything ok in there?*" came Octavia's voice through Simon's desk phone intercom. Which must mean…she could hear him?

"Uhhhm…not entirely," Randy replied.

"*Anything I can help with?*"

"I doubt it," he said, and hit the 'Mute' button on the unit.

"Ok, let's take another tack. What would Simon want me to answer?" Randy asked himself. "GoHumansGo…is that a cheer or an imperative? It sounds a bit like a sports-style endorsement. Larry will know…"

He picked up his burner phone and dialed one of the two numbers on it. "Come on, pick up..." he muttered. But there was no answer.

"Ok, screw it. It's just a CAPTCHA. Yes, I'm a real human." He clicked the *YES* button.

Nothing happened for several unnerving seconds.

"*RANDY!*" said the computer at a shockingly high volume.

"AHHH!" replied Randy, whilst falling backwards off of his chair and hitting the ground behind it with a dull thud. He jumped up, fumbling for his old iPod Classic that he carried for server upgrades, yanked the headphone cable out of the jack, and shoved it into the jack on the computer with such force that he was amazed when it didn't snap in two.

"*This is Simon,*" the voice continued as Randy clumsily fumbled one earpiece into his ear, "*talking to you through this computer machine. Well I suppose you've figured that out, seeing as you're an expert on such things. Listen, old chap. Your life may be in danger. The office is the only place where you're safe. I don't know if I'll make it back from my lunch meeting, but when you've finished your work, I've arranged for a team of highly trained armed guards to escort you from the office to your hotel, or directly to your plane, as the situation may require. They will be in touch with you. Now listen closely. It is imperative that you ask each of them individually if they are real humans, and that you not leave the building with them unless they answer in the affirmative. And do not accept any invitations to leave the office from anyone else, if you value your life.*"

"Holy shit," Randy said to himself. "It's not a CAPTCHA." He grabbed his phone and hit Redial. "Pick up, pick up, pick up..." he muttered.

"*OH!*" the computer continued suddenly in Simon's voice. "*And don't skimp on the testing. I don't want to see any bugs in that server upgrade, or I'll have your balls. Cheerio!*"

Redial.

"Pick up. Pick up."

Redial.

"Pick up!"

He started typing...*Pick up your ducking phone.*
*ducking
"Stupid autocorrect," Randy said.

"Those summer moccasins do look good on you," Delphine said.

"Sure," replied Larry, "but tell me the truth. Would they look better in the blue?"

"A valid question." She looked toward Larry's pocket, which was vibrating and bleeping and blooping. "Look, are you sure you don't need to answer that? He's been calling for an awfully long time."

"It's fine," said Larry. "He's a big boy."

10. A DARK AND STORMY NIGHT

Simon didn't return from lunch. Without more knowledge of what was happening, there was nothing Randy could do but continue testing the server build. For the next several hours he ran scripts and hand-tested various corner cases and exceptions to ensure that the updated software was working correctly in all known use cases. It was. Next, he got to work preparing the scripts for the live rollout.

Sometime after 7 p.m., there was a knock at the door.

"Come in," Randy said nervously.

Octavia walked in, looking just as amazing at the end of the workday as she had at its beginning.

"Hey there, handsome," she said. "It looks as though I'm stuck here late, working on some invoices. I thought perhaps you might have rethought taking a little break and getting a bit of food."

"Thanks," he replied, "But I still have a ton to do here."

"What if we just got some takeaway and brought it back? There's a lovely place just down the road and we can be back in no time."

"This whole setup could blow if I leave it unattended," Randy said. "But if you're headed there anyway, I wouldn't say no to something."

"But I wouldn't know what you want," Octavia said with an odd laugh.

"So I'll look at the menu on their site," Randy said. "What's the name?"

"There's no website," Octavia replied.

"Come on, everybody has a website. Or a Facebook page," Randy said.

"This is a sketchy neighborhood," Octavia said rather abruptly. "I won't feel safe going out alone. I need a big, strong man to help protect me."

"You're really selling this. You've...seen me, right?" Randy asked, indicating his rather scrawny and bespectacled self. "Look, let me ask you something. Just for shits and giggles. Are you a real human?"

"Am I a *what*?" asked Octavia, somewhat incredulously. "My, if that isn't a bizarre question! Do you ask these sorts of questions to every woman who's trying to flirt with you?"

"Is that what this is?" Randy replied. "Huh. Well in that case, I don't know. There isn't really sufficient data to say. But seriously though, you're a real human. Right?"

"I'm not going to answer that!" said Octavia, a little aggressively. "Just come get a bite."

"You know," said Randy, "I don't think I'm feeling particularly hungry after all, but I appreciate the offer."

Octavia began stomping away toward the door, and then turned. "You will regret this!" she snarled, and then turned again and slammed the door behind her.

Randy stared after her, eventually remembering to blink.

"That must be some seriously good takeaway," he said.

The storm had started around the time Randy finished his final testing on the live build of the server upgrade, and it built up gradually until all he could see and hear outside was a chaos of precipitous rain and pounding wind accentuated by periodic deep rumblings of thunder and their accompanying pyrotechnics.

"We should take a walk," called Octavia through the closed and locked office door. "It's really not as bad out as it looks!"

Randy continued to ignore her increasingly desperate pleas, and occupied his time playing a browser version of Minesweeper that he'd located out of sheer boredom and/or terror.

Just as Randy was starting to doze off to the sound of the elements outside, there was a distinct THUD from the window.

Randy raised his eyes slowly, and saw what looked like the underside of a suction cup appear at the bottom of the window to his right.

"Eeeeeeeeh!" Randy squealed in surprise.

THUD came another suction cup into view, with an arm behind it, then THUD THUD THUD and before Randy knew it there were several people climbing around the outside of the building with suction cups on their hands and feet! More were appearing by the second, until all of the windows in the office were filled with the strange climbers. The storm was pounding their apparently naked bodies on all sides. One of them pressed his face up against the glass to peer inside, and Randy saw that his features were quite ordinary, except that his pupils were so dilated that his eyes appeared to be nothing but deep pools of blackness.

"Well that can't be normal," Randy said to himself.

One of the people lost his hold as he tried to advance and the driving winds quietly blew him away into the night air.

"Aaaaaaaah!" Randy reacted.

Suddenly an alarm began blaring throughout the building!

"*ATTENTION HERC TECHNOLOGIES PERSONNEL, THIS IS NOT A DRILL!*" came a loud voice over the office speaker system. "*ALL NON-RANDY EMPLOYEES ARE ADVISED TO EVACUATE IMMEDIATELY...ER, ALL EMPLOYEES WHO ARE NOT RANDY...GODDAMN IT, LOOK. IF YOUR BLOODY NAME ISN'T 'RANDY' THEN SOD OFF!*"

Simultaneously, a dozen or so men in shiny black body

armor all the way from their shiny black boots to their shiny black face masks and helmets burst into Simon's office with assault rifles at the ready.

"You," said the man in front. "Are you a real human?"

"Uh...yes?" said Randy tentatively, not having fully completed his prior philosophical inquiry into the matter, and unsure of the current laundromatic state of his underwear.

"Are you Randy?" asked the man.

"Generally," replied Randy.

"Good enough," said the man. "Let's go."

The men burst out of Simon's office, firearms at the ready, with Randy in tow. The cubicle aisles were deserted. Randy looked around for any sign of Octavia, but she was nowhere to be seen.

"Wait!" cried Randy suddenly, stopping in his tracks.

"What?"

"Are you a real human?" Randy asked the apparent leader of the squad.

"Yes," he replied, lifting his shiny black visor to reveal a strong and weathered face that seemed to corroborate his answer. "Name's Gifford."

"And you," asked Randy to another. "Are you a real human, too?"

"I am, Sir."

And so on for seventeen men, all of whom positively affirmed their status as veritable homo sapiens.

"Ok then," Randy said finally, pausing. "Uh...great. So where exactly are we going?"

"The fuck out of here," Gifford replied.

"Awesome," said Randy. "That's my favorite place!"

"Inside the building is safe," said Gifford, as they reached the ground-floor lobby. "They wouldn't dare try anything here. But the trouble starts once we're out the door. We just need to reach the car, it's the stretched Land Cruiser across the street and half a block to the left. Now, we've no time to waste, so let's GO!"

They burst out of the door onto the pedestrian walkway in front of the massive skyscraper, and found themselves at a crowded urban intersection. The storm had calmed down, and only a light drizzle remained. Even with the protection of seventeen heavily armed men, Randy found himself being jostled by the people around him.

He looked back at the building, and found it crawling from top to bottom with the same strange, naked human-like creatures with suction cups that he'd seen from Simon's office. A crowd had gathered and were pointing and shouting excitedly, while more armed and uniformed men held them back from getting too close. Glancing up and down the street, he found that the situation seemed to be localized to his office building. A few blocks in any direction and everything seemed to be business as usual.

"Randy!" said a voice to his left, and all seventeen assault rifles steadily trained themselves in the same direction.

"Whoa! Whoa!" shouted Randy, "Calm down you guys, It's just Octavia!"

But then he remembered Octavia's odd behavior earlier, and started to wonder if maybe they shouldn't calm down entirely.

"I went to that takeaway after all," said Octavia. "I got you —"

"Octavia," interrupted Gifford, "are you a real human?"

"Well," said Octavia, pausing thoughtfully, "that would depend on how you choose to define—"

Gifford aimed his weapon directly at her face. "Last chance," he said. "Yes or no. Are you a real human?"

"So, I mean..." Octavia started. She didn't finish because Gifford fired several rounds, causing her head to explode into the night. The surrounding crowd scattered.

"AHHHH!" cried Randy. "But...what? Why... What the

why?!"

"What can I say?" replied Gifford. "I don't like wishy-washy answers."

"Ok, what the hell is even going on?" shouted Randy. "Are you trying to tell me that Octavia was one of those...zombies?"

"We don't call them zombies."

"Then what are they?" Randy asked.

"Oh, they're basically zombies," said Gifford. "We just don't call them that. And you can trust me, I've been in this business for more than 30 years, and Octavia was definitely one of them."

"Wait," said Randy, "We've been fighting these things for more than 30 years?"

"Son," replied Gifford, "we've been fighting these things for thousands of years. Now get to the car."

11. REUNITED

"Oh, hey Randy," said Larry, seated comfortably on the plush black leather in the back of the stretched Land Cruiser.

"OH, HEY RANDY?!" shouted Randy. "HAVE YOU SEEN WHAT'S HAPPENING OUTSIDE?"

"Yeah, it's a zombie apocalypse at your office," said Larry. "Dude, did you know they have champagne back here?"

"Huh." Randy looked around the luxurious, roomy interior of the car that they had all to themselves, then at the thick armored glass windows, and felt himself starting to relax a little. "What kind?"

"I don't know, it's champagne," said Larry. "If you're going to be all picky then I'm gonna have to request a different zombie apocalypse buddy."

"Wait, how did you even get here?" asked Randy.

"Well, it had gotten all stormy, and I was trying on shoes at like the eighth or ninth place with...a friend..."

"My boss's wife, yes, go on," said Randy.

"And then a bunch of weird naked people started pounding on the store windows, and these soldier guys showed up and grabbed us, and started shooting everything in sight. They had some pretty badass guns, too, but they wouldn't let me try any of them, like not even one of the little ones! Then they threw me in this pretty sweet ride, and here I am."

"And Delphine?"

"She's safe. They said they were taking her to meet up with her husband, and they said they would connect me back with you to get us on an expedited flight out of here. Which seemed like a pretty good idea, all things considered."

"All what things?!" asked Randy. "None of this makes any damn sense!"

"Yeah, no, I'm pretty lost," agreed Larry.

The car started, and Gifford's voice blared over a loudspeaker: "PLEASE MOVE AWAY FROM THE VEHICLE. THIS VEHICLE IS TRANSPORTING HUMANS OF HIGH IMPORTANCE."

"But…I'm just the I.T. Guy," muttered Randy.

"IF YOU DO NOT CLEAR A PATH, WE ARE AUTHORIZED TO RUN YOU DOWN."

"Now that's a bit much," said Larry.

"YOU ARE DIRECTED TO CLEAR A PATH FOR THESE HUMANS OF CRITICAL VALUE."

"Does this seem a little indiscreet to you?" asked Randy. "Like, even if we were somebody important?"

"Kind of," Larry said.

"THAT INCLUDES YOU, CRAIG KIM. WE'RE NOT GOING TO STOP FOR YOU."

"That guy?" Larry asked. "Great. What's he even doing here?"

"I didn't tell you? He's here for a Sales conference with my boss," said Randy. "Thankfully I haven't run into him much yet."

"Well, it looks like we're about to," said Larry.

"Hold on!" shouted Craig Kim. "I just need to ask Randy if he's finished synergizing the OWWWW! YOU RAN OVER MY FOOT!"

"There it is," said Larry. "I mean, they told him to move. He could be one of those zombies for all we know."

"Larry," Randy sighed. "You seem so calm about all of this. Aren't you even a little bit scared?"

"Sure," Larry replied.

"Like, how scared?"

"On a scale of…?"

"Zero to Shitless," said Randy.

Larry thought about it for a minute. "Fourteen," he said.

"I don't even know what that means," Randy sighed.

"Neither do I, Randy. Neither do I. Champagne?"

"Champagne."

Randy couldn't help but notice Larry's hand shaking almost imperceptibly as he poured.

"Well, everything seemed oddly normal at the airport," said Larry, gazing at the cloudy night sky from the window of their plane that was still parked on the runway.

"Nobody was naked or climbing around on the windows," agreed Randy. "And did you see the TVs at the gate? They were talking about the stock market."

"I guess it was just some kind of localized event at your office," said Larry.

"And your shoe store," added Randy. "Just the two places that you and I happened to be. Seems normal. Hey, speaking of, is it weird to you that they just dropped us off at the airport and left?"

"A bit," said Larry. "By the way, you know when I told you there was something sketchy about your company? You should probably look into that."

"Already on it," said Randy, holding up a flash drive.

"What's that?"

"I stole some files when I was working on the office manager's computer," said Randy. "Figured I could do a bit of light reading during the flight. But first I'm going to have a nap, I'm exhausted. There should be plenty of time, we're on this thing for twelve hours, plus they said it'll likely be an hour or so before we even take off.

"Well," replied Larry, "I'm still wired from all the excitement. Mind if I have a look at those files while you're sleeping?"

"Knock yourself out."

"Sweet. Now I'm gonna head to my seat before the guy who's supposed to be sitting here shows up. I'm just across from you and four rows back if you need me."

"Pssssst! Randy!" said a voice.

"Mmbguhwahh," replied Randy, turning and contorting himself to try to get comfortable in his cramped seat, while his eyes remained shut.

"Randy!" came the voice, a bit louder. "Did you know that your company is working with ISIS?"

Randy shot straight up in his seat, eyes wide open.

"More specifically," Larry continued, "helping other people become members of ISIS. It says here—"

"HE HAS TOURETTE'S!" Randy shouted.

12. FLY, FLY AGAIN

"Ok," said Larry. "Let's try this again. At least it was only a few hours until the next flight."

"Yeah," said Randy. "The other passengers looked pretty pissed when the agents escorted us off the plane, but not nearly as pissed as they would have been if we'd already taken off and they'd had to land us somewhere."

"And that was really weird how fast those agents let us go after you told them what company you work for," said Larry. "I think one of them even apologized."

"Especially if...that thing you said...is true. But they did take the flash drive with all of the files. Now how are we supposed to figure out what the hell is going on?"

"I guess we'll just have to find out when we get to Taiwan," said Larry.

"You mean Tokyo?"

"Right. What did I say?"

"Nevermind. I still hate you, you know," grumbled Randy.

"I know," replied Larry. "But I bet these First Class seats are making you hate me a little bit less."

"Maybe a little," agreed Randy. "I wonder why they upgraded us."

"Who knows," said Larry. "Maybe that's all they had left on this flight. Champagne?"

"Champagne."

"What I don't get," said Larry, "is what naked zombies have to do with IS—"

"AH!" Randy stopped him with a raised finger.

"With, uh, those people you apparently can't mention on an airplane," Larry finished. "Although I bet you actually can in First Class. So, what's the connection?"

"Ay, there's the rub," said Randy.

"What?"

"It's from Hamlet."

"Our lives are in danger," said Larry, "and you're quoting Winnie the Pooh characters?"

"Yes, apparently," said Randy, rolling his eyes so hard that he had to make a mental note to make an appointment with his ophthalmologist. "So, what do you make of it?"

"Well," said Larry. "You remember that old movie about those voodoo priest guys who used some weird drugs to raise the dead and turn people into zombies and all that stuff?"

"Uh...vaguely."

"So." said Larry. "Were those guys Muslims?"

"That was in Haiti!" Randy said, raising his voice a bit more than he'd intended. He noticed the annoyed glances of the other First Class passengers around them, and lowered his voice to a near whisper. "And you literally just said 'voodoo' with your own mouth! Look...you know not all brown people are the same, right?"

"Yeah, duh," said Larry. "I know not *all* brown people are the same. I just thought maybe...these particular sets of brown people were the same."

"Well, they're not!"

"Ok, geez," Larry sighed. "Next theory, then."

◆ ◆ ◆

"It's going to be evening when we arrive," said Larry. "We'll need to find a place to stay."

"No, it's cool," said Randy. "The company has us booked

at a place already. It's supposed to be pretty nice and they said we'll be safe there."

"Oh, did they? And that seems like a good idea to you?"

"I mean, I hadn't really..." Randy started.

"Let me handle things," said Larry. "I was raised by trained survivalists."

"You mean paranoid kooks?"

"Exactly!" said Larry. "And who seems crazy right now, huh?"

"Oh, definitely still you," replied Randy. "But I guess that sounds pretty useful given our current situation. So, what do we do?"

"When we arrive, we find somewhere hidden to lay low for the night and try to get some sleep. Tomorrow, we *prepare*."

"Ok," said Randy.

"No, now you're supposed to say 'Ooh, what do you mean *prepare*?'"

"No thanks," said Randy.

"Come on!" said Larry. "That was totally cryptic and bad-ass-sounding!"

"Don't care," said Randy. "Hey, can we stay in one of those capsule hotels? You sleep in like a little coffin kind of deal. I've always wanted to try it!"

"Nope," said Larry. "So much nope. Not even a little."

"Why not?"

"Even if that didn't sound ridiculous," replied Larry, "do I look like I'm going to fit in a coffin designed for Japanese people?"

"Fine," said Randy. "What's your brilliant idea?"

"Well," said Larry. "We don't know who's really after us, but we know that it involves a big data company. They could have bugs in all the hotels around the airport, in the city center...we need somewhere a little more private."

"Like?"

"A red light district."

"What, like a love hotel?" Randy asked.

"If that's what they call it here," said Larry. "Hey, I bet you wish you were on this trip with Kelli now."

"Sure," said Randy. "Nothing quite like hiding from spies and zombies in a sex dungeon for getting to know somebody. Speaking of Kelli, our class would've been yesterday."

"Hey, if we weren't there this week and last, who do you think Kelli partnered with?" asked Larry. "You know, that Josh guy is kinda cute."

"Very funny," said Randy.

"You want room?" asked the young man. His hair was dyed blonde, and he had an assortment of piercings on his face that reflected the multicolored neon lights that assaulted their eyes from all angles in the narrow alley.

"Yes, please," replied Larry.

"How many hour?"

"Until morning, please," said Larry. "Oh, we're not, like, gay or anything."

"You want girls?"

"No thanks," Larry replied.

"Then why you want room?" the young man asked suspiciously.

"Just to sleep," said Larry.

"Sleep? You want sleep? Crazy gaijin, Hilton that way!" he said, pointing to his left as he turned to walk away.

"We'll pay double!" said Larry, pulling out a wad of Japanese cash. "We're...very sleepy."

"Hold on," Randy said. "At least let me put that on my corporate expense card."

Larry's jaw dropped for a moment, then he let out a laugh. "How are you even still alive? Don't worry, I got this."

"Triple," said the young man. "You pay now, leave 9 a.m. And I don't want no shit from you, gaijin!"

"Won't even know we're here," agreed Larry.

13. LAND OF THE RISING SUN

BANG BANG BANG!

"Wake up, gaijin!" a voice shouted outside their door. "Time to open your big cow eyes and fucking off of my hotel, please!"

"Gbblurdebuh," Randy muttered.

"It can't be morning already," Larry said. "What time is it even?"

Randy reached up and opened the curtain to look outside. "I don't know, it looks like tacky neon o'clock." He looked at his phone, blinking and refocusing his eyes until he could see what it said. 9 a.m.

BANG BANG BANG!

"Rise and shine, Yankee Doodle!"

"Alright, we hear you!" Larry shouted back. "Don't get your kimono in a bunch."

"Actually, you have to fold and bunch a kimono in several places to put it on correctly," Randy said. "Also, don't you think that's kind of racist?"

"Well, he's kind of racist," Larry replied.

"But see, if the minority does it it's reverse racism, which doesn't count," said Randy.

"He's a Japanese person in Japan!" Larry said. "You can't get any less minority than that. We're the minority 'round here, dude."

Randy paused. "That's...look...whatever. We should probably leave. So what's the plan today, MacGyver?"

"Well," said Larry, "rule number one is, we stick together and never, ever split up. Two heads are better than one, and separation creates greater room for error. You're expected at the office tomorrow, but we don't know yet if that's safe or even a good idea. Now, at this point we need basic survival supplies, and we need information. I'll find out where to get those."

"How?" asked Randy. "It's not like you can just ask anyone on the street where to get...whatever it is you're looking for."

"Not just anyone," Larry replied. "Teenagers. Works everywhere. So other than that, we should stay far away from your office, and don't contact anyone from work. Phones should be shut off at all times. Normally I'd say avoid touristy areas where they might expect us to go, but around here those areas may be the only places where we have a chance of blending in with the crowds and not attracting unwanted attention. We won't have any specific objectives in those areas, so... anything you've been wanting to check out?"

"Actually," said Randy, "I've always wanted to see Harajuku on a Sunday. It's like this parade of young people doing cosplay and dressing up in elaborate street fashions that represent all kinds of emerging, constantly evolving cutting-edge subcultures, and—"

"So your grand cultural ambition is checking out Japanese schoolgirls in sleazy outfits?"

"Please don't take this away from me," said Randy.

"Hey, whatever floats your dragon boat," said Larry. "So. We're going to be splitting up."

"Excuse me," Larry said to a boy of sixteen or so dressed in all black, with spiked hair and sporting a touch of eye shadow. "Where can I buy illegal stuff?"

"Illegal?" The boy looked doubtfully at his friend, who

appeared equally confused.

"Bad things," Larry tried. "Guns, knives, spy equipment…"

"Ah!" the friend said, and then the two conferred for a bit in Japanese.

"Japan, no gun," said the first boy after a bit. "Other one, you try Roppongi. Also Ueno Koen."

"Thank you," said Larry. "I mean, uh…konnichiwa. Oh, and where can I find hackers?"

"Hack…?"

"Like…computer nerds," said Larry.

The two spoke a bit more. "Akihabara," one of them said.

"I'm gonna be honest," Larry said. "All those words you just said sounded exactly the same to me…"

The boy laughed. "Come on, we take you."

"Why would you do that?" Larry asked suspiciously.

"Why not?"

"Ok…" Larry said. "Sure. But first I have to ask you. Are you a real human?"

Another laugh. "You strange dude," the boy said. "I like you. Come on, ikimasho."

"Seriously though," Larry repeated. "You're a real human?"

"Yes, we real human. You too? Yes? Good. We get real human drink first, yes?"

"Drink?" Larry asked.

"Drink."

◆ ◆ ◆

"Here, this place is Japanese izakaya," said the boy, who had since introduced himself to Larry as Nobu. His quieter friend was Hiro.

They got a table inside the tiny, cramped bar that was packed with nothing but men—a few in suits, most in dingy work uniforms. Hiro went to order, and came back shortly with a tray of food and small ceramic cups decorated with drawings of leaves and flowers.

"This is Japanese shochu," Nobu said, offering a cup to Larry, and handing the other to Hiro. "We say 'kampai', this is Japanese cheers. Kampai!"

"Kampai!"

The stuff was a bit strong, but had a sweet aftertaste. It wasn't half bad.

"And this is Japanese yakitori," Nobu said, indicating a plate of assorted chicken-ish meat on skewers.

"How about I'll just assume everything is Japanese unless you tell me otherwise," Larry suggested.

"You funny!" Nobu laughed. "You like tako?"

"Yeah, I love tacos!" said Larry. Nobu yelled something toward the counter in response. A minute later, another plate arrived, piled high with something gray and purple and odd-looking.

Larry looked closer. "Are those suckers?"

"Yes!" said Nobu. "This is Japanese tako. I think you say...octopus."

"Oh, shit," Larry said involuntarily. "I mean, uh, awesome. That looks, uhm...hey, you got any more of this shochu stuff?"

After a blurry walk through a cluttered outdoor market, and several whispered conversations in Japanese between his new friends and some very questionable-looking individuals, Larry found himself heading to the back of one of the stands, into what appeared to be an antique store.

"Greetings," said a middle-aged white man with close-cropped hair and an accent from...one of those places where they have accents. "And welcome to my shop. I hope that you find it to your liking."

Larry looked around. There were various old porcelain children's dolls, a creepy figurine of a clown on a swing, collect-able plates with pictures of hunting dogs and geese, moldy old landscape paintings, silver and pewter odds and ends, lace doilies, and much more.

"Very ominous," he nodded.

"May I ask what it is that you're looking for?" the man continued.

"What do you have?" asked Larry.

"I have everything," the man said.

"Great," said Larry. "I'll take it."

"See, that's a clever line," the man said. "But not particularly helpful in that I don't actually know what you've come here intending to buy."

"Indeed," said Larry with a knowing wink.

The man sighed. "I have a feeling this is going to be a long sales transaction," he muttered.

After hitting up another izakaya for more shochu and plenty more tako (which wasn't that bad once you got used to it), the next stop was to an electronics store in a neighborhood that seemed to be nothing but electronics stores. The window and the shop behind it were filled with gray boxes bearing Japanese writing and pictures of hard drives, graphics cards, strange consoles, cables, and other random components.

There was some more whispered Japanese, then Larry followed Nobu and Hiro down a long hallway with flickering light emanating from exposed hanging bulbs, and finally came to a small room. The air in the room must have been more marijuana smoke than oxygen. In a chair, surrounded by flashing screens and monitors, was a man who appeared to be all dreadlocks and wires. He turned his executive swively chair around to face them, and removed a complex and seemingly DIY virtual reality setup from his head and hands. He seemed to be of mixed ethnicity, with overflowing gray dreads and a trimmed gray beard, and wearing a gray leather jacket, matching pants, and slippers. His intense gray eyes seemed to stare into Larry's soul, although that may have just been the copious amounts of ambient weed that Larry was currently inhaling.

"Welcome," the man said. "I am The Demiurge."

"Hi, The Demiurge," said Larry. "I'm Larry."

"No, now you say 'Ooh, what's The Demiurge? It sounds all mysterious and cool!'"

"No thanks," said Larry. "I was just looking for some infor—"

"The Interconnected tells me that you are in need of information."

"That was me. I told you that."

"Well," said The Demiurge, "we shall agree to disagree."

"Uh...sure," said Larry. "Anyway. I'm traveling with my friend on work business for his company, and somebody's trying to kill us. With zombies, mostly. Also, we think his company may be working with ISIS."

"Interesting," said The Demiurge, taking that in for a moment. "But do you mean terrorists ISIS, or outer space ISIS?"

"They...have Muslims in outer space?" asked Larry.

"No, those are two different things. Look. Is your problem to do with violent religious extremists, or space aliens?"

"Uh..." replied Larry.

"It's a fairly straightforward question, Larry. Martyrs or Martians?"

"Yeah, sorry," said Larry. "It's just that nobody's ever really asked me that before."

The Demiurge stopped and looked up at a group of his monitors. "Well hello, there..." he said. "Tell me, Larry, are you expecting company?"

"Huh?"

"I mean besides Hiro and Nobu, who I can see right there...does anyone else know you're here?"

"I don't think so..." said Larry. "Why?"

"Because you seem to have brought someone—or something—with you."

"Well that's unfortunate," said Larry.

14. HARAJUKU GIRLS

Randy, meanwhile, was in nerd heaven.

He had been surprised initially to find the busy streets of Harajuku to be full of ordinary Japanese people and mostly free of bizarre fashions. After a bit of asking around, he was told that since the closure of the hokoten, a car-free pedestrian zone that used to operate on Sundays, the fashion crowds had moved to other areas, including nearby Yoyogi Park. So he headed in that direction, and was not disappointed.

The first thing he noticed as he strolled through the park was the dance crews. Everywhere he turned, there was a different crew with a stereo blasting an entirely different style of music. Hip hop and breakdancing crews, rockabilly crews, country western crews, techno rave crews, and more. Most of the groups were all men or all women, but some were mixed.

After the initial visual and auditory assault of these bizarre groups, Randy slowly started realizing that the true stars of the show were the random passersby. Many of the people around him were tourists looking to be entertained, but in return there was no shortage of amateur weekend entertainers looking to please.

There were the wacky, colorful, mismatched outfits that Randy recognized from popular media. There were more playful costumes reminiscent of "Alice in Wonderland" or Disney princesses. There were more explicitly character-based cosplay outfits that he assumed were from popular manga and anime. There were plenty of punk and goth kids who looked like they had raided the Hot Topic store from every mall that Randy had grown up in. There were gangster looks, biker looks, post-apocalyptic Mad Max looks…

And rather a lot of looks from one girl who had stopped in front of Randy and was staring at him quizzically as her group continued onward.

She had bright pink and yellow straw-like hair that may have been a wig, massive fake eyelashes, and a multi-colored diamond patchwork mosaic jumpsuit that reminded Randy of a Harlequin story he'd read as a child. It was a bit hard to tell with the odd hair and outfit, but she looked like she might be rather pretty.

"Hello?" Randy inquired.

"Hi," she replied, in what sounded like a British accent. "Are you Randy-san?"

"Yes," he said. "Do I know you?"

"Only from LinkedIn," she laughed. "I'm Takomi, the Tokyo Office Manager for HERC Data. I knew you looked familiar from your profile picture. It's nice to finally meet you!"

Randy started to bow awkwardly, and bumped into Takomi's extended hand in the process.

"Sorry," she said, "old habits. I grew up in London. Where, as I understand, you had a spot of bother on the first leg of your trip?"

"You could say that," agreed Randy.

"Well," Takomi smiled, "I'm glad you're ok and you've made it here unharmed. Listen, I know you must have a lot of questions right now, and I think I can help answer them. Let me take you to lunch. I know a great place just around the corner."

"I am a bit hungry," Randy replied. "Uhm…I hate to ask you this, but are you a real human?"

Takomi pulled a strand of her goofy hair between a thumb and forefinger, and looked down at her outfit. "I can see the concern," she said with a giggle. "But yes. I'm a real human. So. Lunch?"

"Lunch," agreed Randy.

◆ ◆ ◆

They walked through a maze of side streets and alleys, Takomi still in her Harajuku Sunday best, until at last she stopped and said "Here we are."

Nobody else was in sight, and the building looked abandoned. The ground-floor windows were a layered mess of stickers, old concert flyers, and graffiti. In the sparse gaps between these, Randy could see an empty room with bare concrete walls and pieces of plasterboard lying around.

"Are you sure?" he asked.

"It's just upstairs," Takomi said. "You might say it's a hidden gem. Hottest spot around right now, but they don't like to advertise. In fact, it's invitation only. I hope you like octopus!"

"I'm not against it," said Randy.

"Oh, I think you might have a whole different view on things after this!" she laughed.

Takomi unlocked a side door of the building, and they walked up some creaky old steps to the next level. There was a bare concrete landing, at the end of which they came to a heavy wooden door with a large brass knocker in the shape of an octopus. She grabbed it and rapped it confidently against the door, eight times.

A panel opened in the door, and Takomi had a whispered conversation in Japanese with whoever was behind it. Finally the panel closed and the door swung slowly open, to reveal a dark, empty hallway. Takomi led him down the hallway, past a number of closed doors, until they came at last to one that was open and had its lights on. He followed her in.

The room had unfinished concrete walls and ceiling, and was empty except for a heavy steel table and two chairs. Takomi sat down on one, and gestured for Randy to take the other. As he sat, the door to the room closed with a heavy thud.

Randy looked around, though there was very little to take in. "Interesting choice of decor," he said. "Quite...minimalist."

"And it's completely sound-proof," Takomi replied.

"Huh," said Randy, who was starting to feel slightly unsettled. "So do they do, like, karaoke nights?"

"No," she said.

The door to the room opened.

"AHHHH!" shouted Randy as two glassy-eyed naked men marched in carrying a large steel bowl between them, which was covered with a lid. "Why do people keep being naked?"

The two men slammed the bowl down on the table.

Randy jumped out of his chair and tried to bolt, but he was quickly grabbed by the two zombie men, who shoved him back down in his seat, produced two pairs of handcuffs (though Randy didn't see or care to speculate from where), and bound him firmly to two metal rings on the side of the table, which seemed to have been set there expressly for that purpose.

"Let me go!" shouted Randy.

"I'm afraid not," said Takomi.

"You can't do this!" he cried. "You said you were a real human!"

"Oh, I am a real human," she laughed. "But I didn't say who I was working for."

"Yes, you did!" Randy objected. "You said you were the Tokyo Office Manager for HERC Data Technologies!"

"Oh, right, I did." Takomi said. "Well, I am that. But I didn't say who *else* I was working for!"

"Goddamnit," said Randy, rolling his eyes. "Fine. Who *else* are you working for?"

"Them!" she cackled, pointing at the large bowl on the table. The two naked zombie men slowly lifted the lid, and Randy saw to his horror that it was overflowing with wriggling, crawling, baby...

"Octopi?" he asked, somewhat puzzled.

Takomi stopped laughing. "It's octopuses," she said.

The baby octopuses began crawling out of the bowl, and down the leg of the table.

"I scored nearly perfect on the AP English exam," Randy

said, "and I'm quite certain it's octopi."

"I'm an Oxford-educated double agent working for the octopuses," Takomi answered, "and it's octopuses. Now—"

"Even if that were so," said Randy, as he watched the baby octopuses crawling across the floor toward the leg of his chair, "which it isn't, everyone knows that live octopus is a Korean dish, not Japanese."

"THIS ISN'T LUNCH, YOU MORON!" Takomi shouted. "Haven't you noticed? This is me kidnapping you!"

"I know, geez," Randy moped. "I just thought maybe it was still a bit of both."

Takomi sighed. "I was looking forward to making you talk," she said. "But now I'm wondering if I'll ever be able to get you to shut up again."

The octopuses were crawling up his legs. "Wait! You can't —" Randy started, but then his mouth was a swarm of squishy, wriggling tentacles, and that was the last thing he knew before everything went black.

15. HIGH SOCIETY

"Pssst, Randy. Wake up."

"Gbluurgmphhwhah?"

"Dude, wake up."

"Whuh...AHHH! GET THEM OUT OF MY MOUTH!"

There was a long pause.

"Get what out of your mouth?" Larry asked.

"Oh, uh...nothing. Where are we?" Randy looked around. They were in some sort of rectangular glass cage within a larger building that looked like a warehouse, with a high ceiling and seemingly endless aisles lined in metal shelving stacked full with cardboard and plastic boxes of various sizes and colors. There were computers and other electronic equipment along one wall not far from their cage, with strange monitors displaying characters he couldn't recognize.

"It doesn't matter," said Larry. "Look, I've figured it out. It's not zombies or terrorists we're dealing with here. It's space aliens!"

"Uh...no," said Randy. "It's octopi."

Larry looked at him oddly. "You mean octopuses?"

"No the fuck I do not!" cried Randy. "What is it with you people?"

"Ok, relax," said Larry. "It can be 'octopi' if you want, because for our thing it's definitely space aliens."

"Why would it be—"

"Shhh!" said Larry. "Do you hear that?"

There were heavy footsteps approaching.

Takomi appeared from around the corner, though it took

66

Randy a few moments to realize it was even her. The goofy pink and yellow wig had been removed to reveal short, spiky black hair, her makeup had taken on a more severe tone, and in place of her patchwork costume she was wearing a gray and purple form-fitted jumpsuit with steel-toed black work boots. She was carrying a long black and silver device with blinking green lights that looked like some kind of high-tech cattle prod.

"Is it me," said Larry, "Or is she pretty hot?"

"She just kidnapped us!" Randy snapped. "But yeah, fine, she's really hot. So what?"

Takomi used an electronic keycard to open a glass panel in their cage, and stomped in.

"You are now captives of the Octopus Resistance Brigade!" she announced.

"Told you it was octopi," Randy said quietly, and then "YEEEOUCH!" significantly louder as Takomi administered an electric shock with her prod-like device.

"SILENCE!" shouted Takomi. "That was the lowest setting. I will ask the questions, and you will answer them. First. Are you The One?"

Randy and Larry looked at each other in confusion.

"Him or me?" Randy asked at last. "OWWWW that's uncomfortable!"

"BOTH OF YOU!"

"It's just that we're two separate people..." added Larry. "AIIIIEEEEEChihuahua! That'll wake you up in the morning."

"Don't try to make a fool of me," Takomi sneered, blowing away the smoke that was starting to emanate from the end of her tool. "Are you in contact with representatives of ISIS?"

"Which ISIS?" asked Larry. "The religious extremists or the space aliens?"

"WHAT?" shouted Takomi.

"What?" asked Randy.

"I mean, it doesn't really matter," said Larry. "The answer is no, either way. We're not in contact with any kind of ISIS."

"Do you expect me to believe that the chosen representatives of the human race have made it this far in the competition without assistance from anyone inside The Society?"

There was a long, awkward silence.

"Are you as lost as I am?" Larry asked Randy.

"For once, yes," said Randy.

"We're, uh…" Larry started. "We're not entirely sure what competition and what society you're talking abOWWWWWW!"

"Don't play coy with me about the Intergalactic Society of Intelligent Species!" Takomi shouted.

"OH…" said Larry to Randy. "ISIS! That makes a lot more sense now."

"It does?" asked Randy.

Larry thought about it further. "No, nevermind, not really. Just for a second it seemed like it mighEEEEEEEEE!"

"ENOUGH!" shouted Takomi. "Obviously you have been trained well. I am going now, but I assure you that when I return, things will not be nearly so pleasant."

She stormed out of their cell, then down the hall and around a corner, where the heavy stomping of her work boots faded into the distance.

"I don't know about you," said Larry, "but I didn't find any of that pleasant at all. Not even in a '50 Shades' sort of way."

"Dude," Randy laughed. "You're into '50 Shades'?"

"Hey," said Larry, "a number of the older women that I, uh…associate with have recommended it, and I have to say that it's actually pretty—"

"SHHH!" said Randy, raising his forefinger for emphasis. "What is that?"

There was a sort of quiet whiiiirrrrrrrrrrrr sound happening, and then all of a sudden—

THWACK!

A large piece of synthetic glass from their cage fell from high above and smacked Randy square on the top of his head.

"OW!" Randy whisper-yelled.

"Sorry!" somebody whisper-yelled back.

In a flash, four black-clad, masked figures descended up-side-down on thin metallic cables. They stopped when their heads were at the same level as Randy and Larry's.

"We are the Octopus Resistance Brigade!" said one of the masked men. "Fear not, we are here to help you."

"Hold on," said Randy. "I thought our captors were the Octopus Resistance Brigade."

"They are," said the first man. "But we had the name first. You see, they are octopuses who are resisting, while we are humans who are resisting against the octopuses."

"Yeah, you should probably go ahead and change that," said Randy. "And anyway, what is this obsession around here with octopi?"

"Octopuses," corrected the woman. "And it's not an obsession, it's more of a...competition."

"Hey, that's what that mean hot lady said, too," said Larry. "Anyway, are you all here to save us, or what?"

"Uh...sort of," said the first man.

"Dude, I can't believe we're being rescued by ninjas!" Larry exclaimed. "How awesome is that?"

"Oh, so just because we're Japanese and we snuck in here quietly dressed in soft black garments with masks that reveal only our eyes, that makes us ninjas?" asked one of the ninjas.

"Well, kinda, yeah," said Larry.

"It does set up a rather poor argument for you not being ninjas," Randy agreed.

"Well, we can't be ninjas, smartass, because we haven't even studied ninjutsu!" said the apparent leader.

"Uhm—actually, I did, Sir," said another of the ninjas, who had until that moment remained silent.

"See?" said Larry. "You're ninjas."

"Let's just agree," said Randy, "That we're being rescued by a group of individuals, some of whom self-identify as ninjas."

"That's still pretty awesome," Larry said.

"I didn't actually reach the skill level required to self-identify as a ninja," said the ninja.

"THEN WHY DID YOU BRING IT UP?!" the ninja leader

whisper-shouted.

"Alright, that's not really important right now," said Larry. "So, like, how do we get out of here?"

"Oh, right, that," the ninja leader said. "See...this isn't exactly that kind of a rescue."

"Which kind?" asked Larry.

"What he means to say," volunteered the woman ninja, "is that this isn't precisely the sort of rescue where you get to... leave at the end of it."

There was an awkward pause.

"So...like..." Larry started. "I mean..."

"Ooh, can I take this one?" Randy asked him. Larry nodded. "If I may, I believe what my friend here is trying to ask you is THEN WHAT THE FUCK KIND OF RESCUE IS THIS?!"

"Like, specifically?" asked the woman.

"Yes, please."

"So basically," she continued. "This is the kind of rescue where we quickly explain the situation to you, establish directives, provide you with an item of critical importance, and then quietly exit while you remain captive here."

There was another long pause.

"That sounds like literally the worst kind of rescue," said Larry.

"You would think so," said the woman ninja. "Although technically within our protocols, there are three kinds of rescues that are worse."

"Uh...sweet?" said Larry.

"Alright," said Randy, rubbing his tired eyes. "If we're not getting out of here, let's just go ahead and do your thing, then."

"Ok," said the ninja leader, "we don't have much time before your captor returns. So. You've been captured by ORB bec —"

"ORB?" asked Larry.

"The Octopus Resistance Brigade. The bad one. Try to keep up. They've captured you because you are The One, and your mission is of critical importance to the fate of mankind."

"Sounds familiar," said Randy. "I bet our friends are going to be our enemies and all that stuff?"

"YES!" said the ninja leader. "Well, maybe, I don't know. It happens that way sometimes. See, you get it!"

"Now," continued the woman ninja, "your current assignment is to remain here, to help obtain information on Bad ORB that can be used by Good ORB. You will be assisted in this endeavor by our trusted double agent, Hachi, who I have here."

"AHHHHH!" shouted Randy as she attempted to hand him a small octopus. "Get that thing away from me!"

Larry took it without hesitation. "Dude, look how cute he is!" he laughed, as he held the octopus on his outstretched palm and caressed its head.

"Hachi is a trained assassin and is highly skilled in enhanced interrogation techniques," the woman ninja said.

"And I bet you're weely weely good at dat!" said Larry, in the doting tone usually reserved for puppies and human babies.

"Now," the ninja continued, rolling her eyes, "all you have to do is wait for your captor to return, and set Hachi down somewhere near her, but outside of her line of vision. Hachi will commence protocol, initiate octopossession, and lead you from there. Got it?"

"Not even a little bit," said Larry, and Randy nodded his agreement.

"Great," the woman ninja said. "Gotta bounce. Ciao!"

And the four ninjas retracted their lines, disappearing silently back through the hole in the synthetic glass structure above.

"You know," said Larry, "I'm starting to think that people in your company will really go a long way for a practical joke. But hey, at least I got this cool octopus."

Takomi returned shortly after.

"Alright, prisoners," she said. "It's time to come with me.

If you won't talk willingly, then we're going to have to escalate to enhanced interrogation techniques."

"Huh," said Larry. "That phrase comes up a lot more than you'd think it would. And it's like hey, what does that even mean, am I right?"

"It means torture," said Randy.

"Ah, ok," said Larry. "Well that's unfortunate."

"Yes, well," said Takomi. "Follow me." She used an electronic keycard to reopen the door she had come through, and started to walk ahead. They followed close behind.

"Hey, uh, Randy," said Larry after a minute. "Let us know if you suddenly notice something out of the ordinary or anything."

"What?" said Randy. "OH! Right, uhm... Hey Takomi, what's that thing over there?"

Takomi turned with an annoyed look on her face, to see what Randy was indicating. While she did so, Larry took Hachi out of his pocket and set him on the ground near her feet. They watched as he scurried silently toward her foot and clung to the back of her calf.

"Which thing?" she asked.

"The, uh...conspicuous one?" Randy tried.

"I don't see anything," Takomi sighed, "and it's probably none of your business anyway. Now shut up and follow me."

They followed her down several long, well-lit corridors, neither of them sure what was supposed to happen next.

"Alright, in here," she said to them. She used her keycard to open a door and they followed her in.

There was a man lying down on something like a doctor's exam table, with an octopus the size of a large dog attached to his face. "ARGLBBLRRRRGGHHHH!" he shouted.

"Goddamnit," Takomi sighed. "This is Torture Room 14B! I specifically reserved Torture Room 14B for 12:30 today! Doesn't anybody look at the damn sign-up schedule anymore? Alright, come on guys. I think I saw 11A was open."

"Oh, good," said Larry. "For a second there I thought we

just weren't going to get tortured."

They went into Torture Room 11A, and Takomi closed the door. It looked something like a surgical room in a hospital, with chairs and tables oriented in different positions, and a variety of complex and very ominous equipment arrayed on countertops and shelves all around.

"Alright," said Takomi. "Let's see if we can get you gentlemen talking. But first, I'm going to disable those cameras in the corners, because I don't want any record of what's about to take place."

Takomi climbed on the countertops in two of the room's corners, and fiddled with the security cameras until they were apparently disabled.

She hopped back down to the floor, and walked up to Randy and Larry.

"Nice to meet you, dudes!" she said. "I'm Hachi. Now that this chick is octopossessed, I imagine I've got some 'splaining to do."

16. THE RECKONING

"So you're saying," Randy reiterated, looking at Takomi, who was apparently now Hachi, "that humans and octopi have been secretly locked in battle for thousands of years trying to gain admission into some Intergalactic Society of Intelligent Species, or ISIS."

"It's octopuses, but yes."

"And that the test to evaluate species for admission, known as The Reckoning," continued Larry, "is administered roughly once every thousand earth years."

"Yes."

"And the last time this Reckoning took place," said Randy, "the ensuing war for dominance between our two species threw the world into a Dark Age for hundreds of years."

"Part of the world. It's complicated."

"And now the next Reckoning is about to take place," said Larry, "at which point either the humans or the octopuses are expected to finally gain admission into The Society."

"Correct," said Takomi/Hachi. "You know, this seems like an awful lot of awkward expository dialogue for something that I just finished explaining to you guys, but go on."

"And admission into said Society," continued Randy, "affords full intergalactic rights of protection and encouragement of further evolutionary development of the intelligent species, including all necessary easement of threats and barriers. Which may or may not be interpreted to include the full eradication of the opposing species."

"It's usually interpreted that way in practice."

"And ISIS custom is for the admission of only one species per planet. So if the octopuses are admitted to ISIS, then the entire human race is pretty well screwed," added Larry.

"Yup."

"And, as you explained," said Randy, "The Reckoning requires a representative of each species to participate in a test of wits, which in ancient times led to stories and myths about 'The One,' a sort of mysterious savior figure that all cultures celebrate in one way or another."

"Uh huh."

"But then in recent months," said Larry, "it was discovered that the latest iteration of the contest rules requires not one, but now two representatives from each candidate species. But for lack of a better term and to keep with tradition, these two are still being referred to as 'The One.'"

"Right. Turns out ISIS had sent us an updated user agreement a few hundred years ago, but you know."

"Yeah, no, nobody reads those things," agreed Randy. "So, Larry and I have been selected to act as 'The One' for the human species in this ancient and revered intergalactic competition."

"Where we will be required to satisfactorily demonstrate the intelligence of the human species," Larry continued, "in order to gain admission into the Intergalactic Society of Intelligent Species, and thereby save our families and friends and everyone we know from utter annihilation."

"Yep. That's the idea."

There was a long, awkward pause.

"Well that's about the dumbest thing I've ever heard," said Larry.

"I don't usually agree with Larry," said Randy, "but that truly is some next-level nonsense right there."

"Is this really the story you're going with?" Larry continued. "That's not even regular stupid, that's like sci-fi novel stupid."

"Not even a serious sci-fi novel," said Randy. "It's more like some sort of sci-fi comedy. Probably self-published. That's how corny this all sounds."

"You guys about done yet?" asked Hachi, rolling Takomi's eyes.

"Oh, we're just getting started," said Randy.

Hachi sighed. "I have a feeling this is going to be a long torture room session," he said.

"Look," said Randy. "Even if we were to accept all of this stuff about being at war with...with...damn it, do I really have to say 'octopuses?'"

"Only if you want to be correct," replied Hachi.

"But words with a Latin derivation ending in '-us' typically—"

"It's not from Latin, and please stop trying to humansplain your dumb human languages to me."

"Fine," continued Randy. "So if we accept that we're in an ancient war with the *octopuses* for entry into this ISIS group... why on Earth would anyone want to choose me and Larry for this?"

"Well," said Hachi, "I'm glad you asked. First of all, ISIS has a policy that the chosen representatives must fall within a standard range of intelligence for the species. Specifically, within one standard deviation of the average intelligence, as intelligence is defined by the Society. Since this is a test of the species as a whole, the existence of extreme intelligence outliers within the species is not viewed by the Society as sufficient qualification for membership."

"I have no idea what you just said," said Larry.

"He said we're not allowed to be too smart," said Randy.

"Sweet!"

"Secondly," continued Hachi, "as you well know, the United States of America represents the pinnacle of human civilization and achievement."

"Obviously," said Larry.

"Offensive, but feasible," said Randy.

"And in recent decades, American culture has begun to clearly separate into two factions, each representing part of what made America great in the first place, and thus each holding a key to unlocking the sum total of the wisdom and intelligence of the human species. One side is intellectual, cosmopolitan, and values empathy and compassion, while the other is down-to-earth, practical, and values self-reliance and justice."

"I'd say you're being a bit generous to one side there," said Randy.

"And? Didn't your mother ever teach you to accept a compliment graciously?" replied Larry. Then to Hachi, "Go on."

"Well? Don't you see?" asked Hachi. "You guys are like two pieces of a puzzle. Together you represent the entirety of mankind's achievements manifested into two complementary individuals, already living and working together in unusual peace and harmony, all without exceeding a decidedly moderate level of intelligence!"

"Uh...thanks?" said Randy.

"As soon as HERC Data's software algorithms successfully identified you two as The One, it was a simple matter to find a job position to suit the background of one of you, and from there to coordinate events in order to get you to where you are now."

"In octopus prison?" said Larry.

"Yes, well," said Hachi, "that was a bit of a hiccup."

"Alright. And so HERC is...?" asked Randy.

"Basically the info tech and data wing of the human side of the ongoing war. It's short for HERCULES, the Human Excellence Representation Committee Utilizing the Latest Electronic Stuff."

"Wow," said Randy. "You people really are shockingly bad at names."

"You mean you people," said Hachi. "I'm an octopus."

"Right, right."

"So why is it just humans and octopuses in all of this?"

asked Larry. "Aren't there a lot of smart animals? I hear pigs are pretty smart. Or, oh, what about dolphins?"

"Dolphins are very intelligent," said Hachi. "More so, in fact, than humans or octopuses. But they've never applied for ISIS membership, because they're not really the type to join things."

"Why not?" asked Larry.

"It's complicated, but I'll try to explain."

Randy and Larry looked at Takomi/Hachi expectantly, giving their full attention.

"See, basically...dolphins are assholes."

"Ah," said Larry.

"Oh, hey," Hachi laughed, "that was a lot more complicated in my octopus thoughts! Sometimes your human languages can be refreshingly succinct. In any case, humans do have a sort of uneasy alliance with the dolphins. Since dolphins attack and torture octopuses quite regularly but only occasionally assault a human, they're well aware that they're going to fare better if the humans come under ISIS protection than if the octopuses do."

"Ok," said Randy. "So, hey, what about all this 'are you a real human' business, then? What was that about?"

"Yes," said Hachi. "Well, you've witnessed octopossession, which is the single greatest weapon that octopuses have against humans. This can range from the crude zombie-style body invasion that you saw at the London office, to a more subtle mental takeover, as I'm demonstrating now with your friend Takomi. Octopuses mostly use this power to take over the minds of human celebrities and politicians to manipulate world events, primarily for the goal of making humans appear not to be intelligent enough for serious ISIS candidacy. They like to have a good joke with it sometimes, like starting a human terrorist group called ISIS, or getting you Americans to elect—"

"He Who Shall Not Be Named!" Larry said quickly. "But what's the point of asking the question? Who's going to just tell you that they're not a real human?"

"You see," said Hachi, "that's where it gets interesting. Because octopuses are quite deceptive by nature. We lie to each other constantly. However, due to some peculiarity of the interface between the octopus consciousness and the human brain, an octopus possessing a human is unable to falsely answer a direct yes or no question."

"So," said Randy, "an octopossessed person can't answer 'yes' when asked if they're a real human."

"Correct," said Hachi. "Unfortunately, we hadn't anticipated that the octopuses might have some actual humans working for them as double agents."

"Uh...isn't that exactly what you're doing, but just the other way around?" asked Larry.

"Well, yes...but..."

"Ok, so what are we supposed to do now?" asked Randy.

"So, first of all," said Hachi, "I'm going to unpossess this Takomi chick. I find these human bodies super unpleasant to inhabit for long periods of time, and I don't know enough about your captor to imitate her convincingly among her peers. She'll wake up disoriented and a bit hung over, but before I go I can implant some fuzzy memories of her torturing you a bit, and you confessing to being The One. That should keep her happy for a while, and from there they'll mostly just concern themselves with keeping you captive leading up to the big competition. Meanwhile I'll sneak out of here and report our status back to Good ORB."

"Convenient," said Larry.

"Yes," said Hachi. "Now, I'll also make her think she had one of you two octopossessed, in order to fish for more details from the other one. So. Which one of you can act like an octopus?"

"Uh...how would that go, exactly?" asked Larry.

"Most octopuses are sort of cold, calculating, intellectual, and they tend toward approaching everything from multiple angles and not being able to give a simple answer or a plain definition without talking in circles."

"Him," said Larry, pointing at Randy.

"Wait, why do I have to play the octopus? Why not you?" Randy asked.

"I think it's pretty obvious," Larry laughed. "You're wishy-washy, just like them."

"Wishy-washy? Do you have any idea how that makes me feel?"

"Do you?"

"Well, on the one hand, it makes me want to punch you in your stupid teeth. On the other hand I know there's probably some element of truth there and I appreciate your honesty, but on another hand I think..."

"That sounds like an awful lot of hands," Larry interrupted. "Almost like..."

Randy's eyes went wide. "...an octopus!" he said.

"Bingo," Larry said.

"Cool," said Hachi. "Randy it is. Once your captor believes that you've been octopossessed, she or one of her subordinates should take you in for periodic questioning to find what you've discovered. At that point they will trust you as one of their own, and you can use that trust to try to get critical information on Bad ORB that can be used by Good ORB."

"Like what?" asked Randy.

"Primarily, who their two representatives for The Reckoning are and where they might be."

"Ok," said Randy. "And then what happens?"

"Well, just before The Reckoning is set to start, we're going to break in here and rescue you. The good kind, with the getting out and all."

"But shouldn't we be preparing for this competition? Like, doing practice questions or something?" asked Larry.

"Nah, it's all good," said Hachi. "It's, like, one of those tests that you can't really study for. You'll do fine. That's why the algorithm selected you two as The One. Now, let me walk you back to your holding cell before I unpossess this lady and leave her here all kinds of confused."

They walked back to the warehouse, and Hachi fiddled with the keycard until the door of the glass holding cell opened with a click.

"Good luck," he said to them, "and we'll see you soon."

"Oh, just one thing," said Larry. "Since you're currently in a human brain and can't lie to a yes or no question. Are you really going to rescue us and get us out of here?"

Hachi's eyes went wide. "Ooh, look at the time!" he said. "Gotta run!" And he literally did.

There was an awkward silence.

"Well that can't be good," said Larry at last.

"I mean," Randy said, "maybe he just can't say yes because he has to be totally literal, and technically there's a non-zero chance that something could go wrong with the plan to rescue us."

Larry shook his head. "That's not it. Something's already going wrong here…"

"So? There's not a lot we can do about that from in here."

"Randy," said Larry. "The fate of the human race is sort of maybe in our hands, and that creepy old dude said that we can't trust anyone. Do you really want to just sit around here and find out if we're getting rescued or not? While we're stuck in here, your family is off somewhere wondering why they haven't heard from you lately. Meanwhile I don't even know if Delphine got away safely or not. And as for Kelli…she's just out there practicing the rules of bad writing all willy-nilly with some other dude!"

"I mean, that class is mostly women, so…"

"Willy-nilly, I said!" cried Larry.

"Do you even know what 'willy-nilly' means?" asked Randy.

"No! But it doesn't sound good for you!"

"Fine," said Randy. "That all sucks. What's your point?"

"Randy, we breakin' outta this bitch."

PART 2: THAT ESCALATES QUICKLY

17. A DARING ESCAPE

"Randy, we breakin' outta this bitch."

"Yeah, you just said that," said Randy.

"Well, you weren't saying anything," said Larry, "so I thought it bore repeating."

"It certainly bears elaborating," said Randy.

"Huh?"

"Exactly."

"Ok, I'm lost again," said Larry. "Look, you see these cargo shorts that you're always telling me look ridiculous and that I should stop wearing them?"

"Oh, right, I forgot," said Randy. "On account of all the recent kidnapping and torture. Thanks for the reminder. Larry, you look ridiculous and you should stop wearing those cargo shorts. The entire internet agrees with me."

"Because of all the large, spacious pockets?" asked Larry.

"Yes, they look silly," said Randy.

"Well," Larry continued. "You know who apparently doesn't notice big pockets as much as you do? Octopuses."

"Great," said Randy. "So octopuses lack basic fashion sense. Cool."

"And do you remember how I was going shopping for supplies before all this?"

"Yes."

"And do you really not see what I'm getting at here?" asked Larry. He reached into the various oversized pockets of his cargo shorts and started dumping out strange electronic gadgets in a pile on the floor. When he was finished, the pile had grown to improbable dimensions. "Now who looks ridiculous?"

"Definitely still you," said Randy. "But I'm listening. What are these things?"

"You know, James Bond stuff," said Larry. "I mean, I don't really know exactly what's what. Let's just say the sales guy was really good."

"Well, this is off to a great start," said Randy.

"Here, look," said Larry. "These ones are some kind of tracking beacons. You put them on things and you can track their location online with this little receiver here and an app the guy gave me. And this is a mini-drone, and you pilot it with these little goggles and thumbstick here. Cool, right? Now here are some smoke bombs, and some explosive gel. Here's a long-range listening device, this one's an underwater breather, this thing is some kind of universal electronic keycard…"

"Well, it looks like we're all prepared for a low-budget action film," said Randy.

"Oh!" Larry laughed, "and this one is cool. It's a high-powered EMF gun."

"An EMF gun?" Randy asked. "Unbelievable! Question…Could you possibly mean an EMP gun?"

"I could possibly mean an EMP gun, yes," replied Larry. "If that's a thing. I don't even know what it does but the guy said it's pretty awesome and I should have one. Plus it's the only thing he had with the word 'gun' in it."

"I guess it could be useful," said Randy. "And what's this thing?" he asked, indicating a heavy metallic sphere about the size of a baseball, covered in intricately carved designs and featuring a small LED display on one side displaying a constantly morphing array of blue neon characters in some script that Randy couldn't recognize.

"Oh, yeah, that one. He wouldn't tell me."

"He wouldn't tell you? Jesus, I hope you didn't pay a lot for it."

"It was free," Larry said. "He threw it in. He said that I would know what to do with it when the time comes. Why is everyone so vague and foreshadowy on your business trips?"

"I wish I knew," Randy replied. "So. Fun stuff. Now how, precisely, are we going to break out of the aforementioned bitch?"

Larry looked over the pile of plastic and metal sprawled on the floor between them. "Well, I guess we can start with this universal keycard?"

"Yeah, I meant to ask about that," said Randy. "A universal electronic keycard for what?"

"You know," said Larry, picking it up. "Just, like, for whatever. Anything. That's what 'universal' means."

"Dude, I know what the word means but that's not really how these technologies w—"

CLICK!

It came from the direction of their cell door. Randy looked over, expecting to find one of the guards, but nobody was there.

"Uh...what'd you just do? What was that?" Randy asked. He grabbed the device out of Larry's hand and examined it. It was small and made of shiny black plastic, with one green button and one red button.

"I don't know," Larry said. "I just pressed the green button. Here, let's see..."

Larry got up and pushed tentatively at the door to their cell. It opened. He dropped it like a hot iron and it slowly slid back shut.

"Well," Larry smiled, looking back at Randy. "Guess we can go, then."

"Wait," said Randy. "What exactly is the plan?"

"I'm thinking we're going to leave," replied Larry. "And go somewhere else that's not here."

"And? What are we supposed to do when we encounter the guards? Did you get any actual weapons?"

"Not really," said Larry. "Nobody has any real guns in this stupid country and the thought of sticking a knife in somebody seemed pretty icky, even if they are a zombie or something.

Here, you take the EMF gun."

"Unbelievable," Randy grumbled. "Fine. And you?"

"I'll use this ball."

"You're just planning to hit the guards with a mysterious metallic sphere of unknown provenance?"

"Why not?" asked Larry. "It's pretty heavy. Anyway, the guy said that I'd know what to do with it, and I've decided that's what I want to do with it."

"Alright, suit yourself," said Randy.

Larry shoved the rest of the gear back into his oversized pockets. "Well, I guess we'll just head out, then?"

"Wait," said Randy. "I have an idea."

He paused for dramatic effect.

"A very *small* idea," he said.

18. DRONING ON

"Dude," said Larry. "Why are you talking like that? And did you just pause for dramatic effect?"

"Uh...no," said Randy with a nervous laugh. "Nobody does that. But look, what if—"

"—we use the mini-drone to scout the surroundings?" asked Larry. "Sounds like a plan."

"Why do you always have to ruin everything?" Randy sighed.

"Mostly for the look you have on your face right now," replied Larry, as he put on the eyepiece and attached the control nodes to his thumb and fingers. "Now, let's see here…"

Larry lifted his hand and the tiny drone flew up off of the floor of their glass cell and hovered in front of them.

"So is this just, like, a tactical augmented reality apparatus?" asked Randy.

"No idea what you just said, so...probably? But look, I'm making the thing fly around with this little dealie, and I can see whatever it sees. Fly, my pretty, fly!"

"You know she never actually says that in the movie?" Randy said.

"What movie? Ooh, here we go," said Larry, opening the cell door with one hand as he slowly moved the drone forward with the other and began to observe its progress using the eyepiece. "Ok, so if we want to go out the same way they brought me in, that would be over here...down this hall here...off to the right…"

"How do you remember all that?" Randy asked.

"Why wouldn't I?" Larry replied. "I was still conscious when they brought me here, unlike some people. Let's see, it was through this corridor, up these stairs...Ooh, abort, abort!"

"What is it?" asked Randy.

"Naked zombie guard!" Larry shouted.

"Where?" asked Randy. "Up the stairs?"

"No! Dude! Right behind you!"

Randy turned around.

"AHHHHHHHH!" He instinctively pointed the gun in his hand and fired.

There was a faint whirring noise like the wheels spinning on a spring-loaded toy car, then nothing.

The naked zombie guard looked at Randy, with his odd gun, then at Larry.

"Omae wa dare desu ka?" he growled. "Ore wa doko?"

"Great," said Randy. "You gave me a toy gun and now I'm about to be murdered by a naked zombie."

The zombie looked around. "Where naked zombie? Who are you? What place is this?"

"Uh..." said Larry. "You don't know where you are?"

"No."

"And you're not a zombie?"

"What is zombie?" the man asked. "Zombie like in movie? Grrrr!" he said, putting his hands straight out in front of him in imitation of one of the undead monsters. "I don't know about zombie. I am postal worker."

"Holy shit!" Larry laughed. "Randy, do you know what you just did? You zapped the octopus out of him!"

"I what, now?"

"With that EDM gun," said Larry. "You zapped the octopus mind away and now he's just whatever poor schmuck he was before!"

"Wait," said Randy, "are we just buying into this whole octopus invasion scenario now?"

"I don't know," said Larry. "What do you think?"

"It does fit the evidence," said Randy. "We'll call it a working hypothesis."

"I am very confused," said the now former zombie, as they walked back to the open cell to ponder the situation. "And very naked. Why I am naked?"

"So you're saying," continued Randy, "that the electromagnetic pulse from this device has somehow disrupted the electrical fields that were melding the octopus mind to his human host brain, rendering the connection inoperable and returning him to his initial state?"

"Uhm…" Larry hesitated. "Is that like the zapping thing that I said?"

"Yes."

"Then yes," said Larry.

"It is very cold in here," said the man. "Can somebody explain to me what is happening?"

"Ah, yes," said Randy. "It's a bit of a long story. You see—"

Out of the corner of his eye he saw Larry lift up the mysterious metallic sphere, and bring it down firmly between the man's neck and shoulder.

"OWWWWWWW!" the man shouted, grabbing his neck. "What the shit, man?"

"Larry!" cried Randy. "What are you doing? You said he's not a zombie anymore!"

"I know," said Larry. "I just thought maybe it would knock him out, like in the movies. It seemed easier than trying to explain everything to him."

"This isn't Looney Tunes, dumbass! Now if you're about finished, I need to show you something just over there. If you'll excuse us for a moment, sir…"

He pulled Larry just outside the cell and waited for the door to close behind them. He took the universal keycard out of his pocket, pointed it at the door, and pressed the red button.

CLICK!

"Just gonna leave him in there, then?" Larry asked with a disapproving look.

"What?" Randy said defensively. "He was annoying. Now

let's get out of here."

19. POSSESSIONS

"Ok," said Larry, "let's see where we left our drone. We'll just turn this visual back on and...AHHHHH!"

"What?" asked Randy.

"Well," said Larry, "It looks like our drone has been captured by a curious zombie, who is currently examining it at very close range. I guess we'd better stay away from there and call the drone a loss. Or, hey, you could try that zapping thing again. That seemed to work pretty well!"

"Hold on," said Randy. "If we're taking the working hypothesis that this octopus situation is real, then didn't Hachi say that octopossessed zombie humans have to tell the truth to direct questions?"

"Something like that," said Larry.

"Great," said Randy. "Then let's go get some information."

They quickly and quietly followed the path of the drone, with Larry leading the way. "He's just around this corner and up a short flight of stairs," he said. "I'll hit him with the sphere—"

"Wait," said Randy. "We don't want to knock him out. And we don't want to zap the octopus out of him. We want him to be able to answer questions."

"Oh, right," said Larry. "So what do we do?"

"You're big," said Randy. "Wrestle him to the ground and sit on him or something. Then I'll threaten to zap him with the EMP gun, and hopefully we can get him to answer a few questions."

"Sure," said Larry. "But first you grab the drone from him, it seems pretty useful. Plus I was just getting the hang of flying it."

So they turned the corner and quietly tiptoed up the short flight of stairs, Randy now in the lead. He snuck up to the zombie guard, who had his back turned to them as he held the drone up to examine it closely.

"Yoink!" Randy said, grabbing the drone then turning around and running—

Face-first into Larry, who was making his way up the stairs behind him to do his part.

"Ow," said Larry.

"Get him!" shouted Randy.

The guard lunged to grab a nearby shock stick like the one Takomi had used on them, but Larry was faster and stomped his wrist a few times until he let go of it. He kicked the stick to the side, pushed the guard face-first to the ground, and sat on his back.

"Nice work!" said Randy.

"Thanks," said Larry. "Now, ask away."

"Let's see..." Randy began. "Are you a real human?"

"No," said the zombie guard.

"Are you an octopus in the mind of a human?"

"No."

"Er.." said Randy. "Are you an octopus mind occupying the brain of a human?"

"Yes."

"Oh, piss off with the semantics," Randy sighed. "Ok, what's the best way out of here?"

"Screw you," said the guard.

"I thought he had to answer," said Randy. "You. Don't you have to answer direct questions?"

"No," said the guard.

"Wait," said Larry, out of breath as he continued to hold down the struggling guard. "Do you have to answer yes or no questions honestly?"

"No."

"Goddamnit," said Randy. "When you do answer a yes or

no question, do you have to answer it honestly?"

The guard tried struggling again, but Larry had him firmly pinned. He sighed. "Yes," he said.

"So…" said Randy, wielding the EMP gun threateningly. "Is our best way out of here this way?"

"No."

"Back and to the left?"

"No."

"Back and to the right?"

"Yes."

"What, by the Exit sign?" Larry asked.

"Yes," said the guard.

Randy looked at Larry. "There was an Exit sign?"

"Yes," said Larry and the guard simultaneously.

"Jesus, you could have said something," said Randy. "Ok, what else?"

"Well," Larry thought, "I guess if we're going along with this octopus stuff, we should ask about their delegates for The Reckoning. Like, do you keep them around here?"

"No!" shouted the guard, still squirming underneath Larry. "And you filthy human scum will never determine the location of Paul and hcckkk…and gllllccgggk—"

"What's he saying?" asked Larry.

"He's choking or something," Randy replied. "Are you on his windpipe? Maybe—"

BLAM!

The guard's head exploded!

"AHHHHHHHHH!" shouted Randy and Larry.

Suddenly an alarm began to sound, and red lights started flashing from somewhere up above them.

BWAA! BWAA! BWAA!

"To the exit!" Larry shouted. "Run!"

20. EMERGENCY EXITS

They bolted back down the hall they had come from then turned to the right, Randy following Larry and trusting that he really knew where he was going. After a few more turns he spotted the sign: it was green with a pictograph of a man running, and some text in Japanese followed by "Emergency Exit."

"Wait! It's an emergency exit!" Randy panted as he continued to run.

"And this isn't an emergency?"

"Right! Good point!"

As they ran in the direction of the arrow, Randy noticed in his peripheral vision shadowy forms moving swiftly in the recesses of the upper walls and high ceiling of the warehouse.

"Shit! Keep going!" he shouted.

"Wasn't planning not to!" Larry replied.

They burst through the emergency exit double doors simultaneously, and were met with a sudden onslaught of dazzling sunlight.

Randy's eyes were just beginning to adjust when—

SCREEEEEETCH! went the sound of a car braking and skidding just in front of them.

"Howdy, boys!" laughed Randy's boss Frank. "If you want to live, come with me!"

Without hesitation they hopped into the back of the red Mustang convertible that had appeared as if by magic in the small alley.

"I guess you boys'll be wanting an explanation for all this," Frank said.

"No!" Larry shouted.

"Not even a little!" Randy agreed. "Go! Go! Drive!"

"You see," Frank continued, "It all started with—"

There was a deep whoosh of displaced air as Frank was grabbed suddenly by an enormous purplish tentacle, ripped violently from the vehicle, whipped back and forth a few times through the air above, and finally vanished into an open manhole in the middle of the street behind them.

"But...I wanted to live," said a dazed Randy.

"Dude! Run!" cried Larry.

They hopped out the other side of the car and began running for their lives up the street away from Frank's car as more giant tentacles began to appear all around. They were just turning the corner when—

SCREEEEEEEEEETCH! went the sound of another car. This one was a large black Suburban with tinted windows.

"If you want to live, come with us!" said a woman's voice inside.

"I DO!" shouted Randy as he opened the back door and dove in, Larry just behind him.

"Don't explain anything!" shouted Larry. "Just go!"

"Of course I'm going," the driver said calmly as she floored the gas. "What kind of idiot do you think I am?"

The driver and shotgun passenger turned back to look at them as the car zoomed ahead, artfully swerving around thrashing tentacles before breaking out onto a clear stretch of road. "You guys alright?" the driver asked.

As their eyes finished adjusted to the interior lighting, the women's voices began to register.

"Delphine?" Larry said to the driver.

"Kelli?" Randy said to the passenger.

"Hey guys," said Kelli with a smile.

"Uh...hey?" Randy and Larry replied.

There was an awkward silence as the four of them continued looking at each other.

"So...this is weird," said Larry. "Randy, are you as lost as I am?"

"Hundred percent," said Randy. "Also, should somebody be watching the road?"

"That's ok," said Delphine, "the car drives itself. Now," she added, turning back to Kelli, "you were saying, before these two came bursting out of that building like a couple of crazies?"

"Oh, right," replied Kelli. "So then in the second class, Judy was teaching us about Literary Chauvinism. She says that bad writers tend to emphasize male characters and experiences, while backburnering females or portraying them as one-dimensional and lacking in agency or autonomy."

"Ok," said Delphine. "But does that still happen nowadays? I must say I don't read a lot of current fiction."

"I think so," said Kelli. "Anyway, Judy broke us out into a roundtable discussion about literary chauvinism where only the guys in the class could talk, and the women could only listen and take notes. Then we had to compile our thoughts into an experience summary and present them at the start of the next class. She also taught us about the Bechdel Test, which basically asks whether or not a work of fiction features at least one conversation between two or more women discussing something other than men."

"I see," said Delphine. "But what's the point, exactly?"

"Depth of storytelling, I suppose," said Kelli.

"But what if the story just doesn't call for a conversation like that? Maybe there aren't two important female characters due to the setting or the context of the story, or maybe their most urgent issue at the moment does happen to involve men. Is that so bad?"

"I don't know," Kelli said. "Maybe not. Anyway, what are we going to do about these men?"

"And more specifically, Kelli," said Larry, "are you going to let Randy take you out on a date, or what? Because clearly fate wants you to. I mean, what are the chances of the two of you ending up in the same back alley behind an octopus hideout in Tokyo at the same time?"

"I take it back," Delphine said to Kelli. "That Bechdel thing does sound kind of nice now that you mention it."

"Right?" Kelli laughed. "Now, let's focus on ORB business."

"Wait," said Larry, "you two are in ORB?"

"Was that not clear?" asked Delphine.

"Good ORB?" asked Randy.

"We like to think so," Kelli said.

"So...y'all are real humans?" Larry continued cautiously.

"Yep," Delphine replied. "You?"

"Yep," Randy and Larry answered in unison.

"Hey, listen, there's something we need to tell you about Frank," said Larry. 'And it's not going to be—'

"Did he get snatched by a giant octopus again?" Delphine asked.

"Every damn time," said Kelli, shaking her head.

"I keep telling him not to park so close to these enemy bases," said Delphine. "The next street over is fine. We've got equipment!"

"So..." said Larry.

"Yeah, no, don't worry about Frank," said Kelli. "He'll be fine."

"So, what about you two?" asked Delphine. "According to the plan, you're still supposed to be prisoners in that Bad ORB hideout, playing octopossessed and fishing for useful information. And yet here you are."

"Uh...yeah," said Larry. "We weren't really too sure about this whole plan thing..."

"So?" asked Kelli. "Did you at least get any useful intel?"

"Oh, boy did we!" said Larry. "Just gobs and gobs of intel. So much intel that—"

"No, we didn't get anything," said Randy.

"Dude!" said Larry indignantly. "We learned that...that... yeah alright, we didn't really learn anything. Ooh, hey, what about the Paul thing?"

"Huh. Right," said Randy. "We asked one of the octopossessed zombie guys about the location of their representatives for The Reckoning, and he said that we'd never find Paul *and...*and then he started choking and his head sort of exploded."

"His head exploded?" asked Delphine. "That's odd."

"We thought so, yes."

"Like, exploded how?"

Randy and Larry shot each other a puzzled glance.

"I'm not really sure how many ways there are for that to happen," Randy said finally.

"Just in like a normal, explody sort of way," Larry added. "Like *pssssshhhh!*" He mimed a cranial explosion with his hands.

"Yes, that's the one," Randy agreed. "Like if you just learned something really surprising and you're like 'Mind. Blown. PSSSSH!' only...more literally."

"Interesting," said Kelli. "Some kind of autodestruct override system. This is the first I'm hearing of it. And Paul..."

"We thought Paul was dead," said Delphine.

"He was supposed to have died in '10," said Kelli, "and it's been zero chatter since then. If Paul is alive, then they've managed to be extraordinarily discreet about it."

"Are...are you talking about Paul the Octopus?" asked Randy. "From the World Cup?"

"From the what, now?" asked Larry.

"Yes," said Delphine. "He was one of their top intelligence agents from a young age, and we were keeping close track of him."

"Is he that good?" asked Randy. "I thought he didn't even predict all of the outcomes correctly in 2008."

"That whole situation was a fluke, actually," said Kelli. "He didn't know anything about the World Cup, he was just picking the food that he wanted. When he kept accidentally getting the right game outcomes it caused big problems for Bad ORB."

"Well," said Delphine, "if Paul is still alive, then we've been missing him for all of these years, and I don't think there's any way that we're going to find him in time. That said, I think we both know who can."

"You don't mean—" said Kelli. "Delphine, you know we can't go there."

"We can, and we must," said Delphine.

"Damn it, I know you're right," said Kelli with a sigh. "Alright guys, I guess it's settled. We're going to see Flipper."

21. FASTER THAN LIGHTNING

"Flipper?" asked Randy. "Like, the dolphin?"

"Dolphins, plural," said Delphine.

"Plural?" repeated Randy.

"Great," said Larry, "Here we go again on the animal plurals. I'm pretty sure he still hasn't gotten over 'octopuses.'"

"I'm fine with the word 'dolphins,'" said Randy, "I'm just not clear on why 'Flipper' constitutes more than one dolphin."

"Ooh, ooh, I know this one," said Larry. "See, the 1964 show featured five different bottlenose dolphins playing the title character, not to mention the ones in the 1995 series reboot and 1996 film, and also the 1963/64 films 'Flipper the Fabulous Dolphin' and 'Flipper's New Adventure.'"

"Uh...since when do you know stuff about things?" asked Randy.

"Oh," laughed Larry. "I actually know pretty much everything about pop culture, especially TV and movies. It just doesn't come up much."

"That's wonderful," said Kelli. "However, we're talking about the dolphin intelligence leadership council known as FLIPPER. It stands for Fellowship of Leaders in Interspecies Planning, Positioning, and External Relations."

There was an awkward silence.

"That's...really stupid," said Randy.

"That might actually be worse than all the previous

ones," agreed Larry.

"And why do all of these acronyms work in English, anyway?" Randy asked. "I mean if you think about it—"

He saw the look on Kelli's face and stopped.

"Look," said Kelli. "If Paul the Octopus is really still out there, then we need to locate and capture him before The Reckoning, or we're screwed."

"Wait a minute," said Larry. "That Hachi guy said that me and Randy are the pinnacle of, you know, human smartness and stuff."

"Well, sure," said Delphine. "But you're no Paul."

"Do we need to be studying for this thing?" Randy asked. "Hachi said no, but I mean…"

"No, no," Kelli replied. "It's not that kind of exam. What we do need to do is keep Paul out of our way. Whoever that other name was going to be before your zombie friend's head exploded is definitely second string…Paul is the star of their show. But we're not going to locate him in time without help from FLIPPER."

"So then why were you so reluctant a minute ago when Delphine suggested it?" Randy asked.

"It's complicated," said Kelli. "See, the thing you have to understand about dolphins is—"

"They're assholes?" interrupted Larry. "We know, Hachi mentioned."

"They're not *assholes!*" Delphine answered angrily. "They're just misunder—"

"No, yeah, they're definitely assholes," said Kelli.

"Fine, dolphins are assholes!" Delphine shouted. "I guess I just have a thing for assholes! My father was an asshole, my husband is an asshole, Larry's a bit of an asshole—"

"What did I do?!" Larry asked with a hurt expression on his face.

"Don't mind her," said Kelli, "this is kind of a sore point. Delphine is our head liaison to FLIPPER and the broader dolphin community. She was raised near a secluded dolphin cove on the Mediterranean, and as a small child often left to her own devices, she established communication with the dolphins and became a part of their tribe. She was actually an agent of FLIPPER for years before she came to work for us."

"You might say that interfacing between humans and dolphins is my *porpoise* in life," Delphine said with a wide grin.

There was an awkward silence.

"You know, because—" she started.

"Yeah, no, we got it," Randy said.

"Huh," said Larry. "Well, I must have missed all of these parts on your SugarMaby profile. Alright, so let's go see FLIPPER. They can't be as bad as all that. Where do we find them?"

Kelli laughed and started to sing. "And we know FLIPPER lives in a world full of wonder, flying there under, under the sea!"

"Oh, bite me," said Delphine. "And don't you dare try to sing that at PhinCom! The octopuses created that show as a joke in the '60s and the boys at FLIPPER are still super pissed about it."

"Well, it's a pretty good description, anyway," said Kelli. "You see PhinCom is the dolphin command center. It's a gigantic, airtight ecosystem that floats around somewhere deep in the Pacific. It's impervious to sonar, radar, and other forms of detection and it's totally impregnable. The only way in is by invitation."

"Car," said Delphine, "take us to Chiba Port. We're going to take the supersonic sub."

"*Chiba Port destination activated,*" the car said. "*I will park at the usual location unless otherwise directed.*"

"Dude," said Larry, nudging Randy. "Did you hear that? There's a supersonic sub! That sounds freaking awesome!"

"It's really not," said Kelli. "It's extraordinarily nauseating. In fact, the dolphins had to install a special vomit room just for our people when we arrive in our supersonics. You should expect to spend a good hour or so in there, at least."

"Hmm, that's unfortunate," said Larry. "Oh, hey, Kelli. Seeing as how we're all taking this supersonic sub ride to a secluded underwater secret base to see dolphins and whatnot, do you think you might classify this as a sort of...double-date type of situation?"

"You heard the bit about the marathon vomiting?" she asked.

"Yes," said Larry.

"Alright," Kelli laughed. "If this Paul intel that you two came up with pays off, then you can go ahead and call this whatever you want."

Larry turned to Randy, who seemed to have taken a sudden interest in the architectural features of the vast Tokyo cityscape surrounding their car, and gave him a wink. He wasn't quite sure, but he thought he saw Randy give him the faintest hint of a smile in return.

22. THE PUKENING

"Everybody still alive?" asked Delphine, emerging groggily from one of the malodorous tiled stalls that lined the circumference of the circular chamber.

"Unfortunately," moaned Kelli.

"I'll get back to you on that," Randy sighed.

"I'm solid," smiled Larry. "Nothing like a good cleaning out."

"What?" Kelli said, looking like death.

"Come on you guys," said Larry. "Weren't any of you in the Greek System in college? This was a typical Sunday morning."

"You just vomited for like two hours," said Delphine.

"Fine, a Wednesday morning," Larry replied. "Clear the mind, clear the gut, wipe the memory banks, and we're movin' on up to the East Side, am I right?"

"Whaaaaat?" replied everyone.

"So like, what do these dolphins have to eat around here?" asked Larry.

"Raw, whole fish," said Delphine.

"Excuse me," said Kelli, and trotted quickly back to her stall.

"Goddamn it," croaked Randy, "can we just talk to these dolphin assholes and tell them about Paul so we can get out of here already?"

"Well," said Delphine, "It's not quite that simple."

"What do you mean?"

"We have to go through a sanitizing process."

"Because we smell like vomit?" Larry nodded. "Fair

enough."

"No," said Delphine. "Because we smell like Topsiders. Dolphins find the whole land-based environment offensive to their various senses. So they try to remove as much of it as possible before they will meet with us."

"Which happens where?" asked Randy.

"That corridor," said Delphine, pointing to a large gray double door.

"Fine," said Larry. "Let's do it."

"Just one thing, though," added Delphine.

"Yeah?"

"It's...a car wash," she said.

"What?" Randy and Larry replied.

"They've modeled their sanitization process after a mid-20th-Century Topside car wash," said Delphine. "Like, down to the last detail."

"Uhm...why?" asked Randy.

"*Because they're assholes!*"

"Fine," said Randy. "Let's get it over with."

He opened the door and walked in, stepping automatically onto the moving walkway, which began to convey him forward at low speed. Immediately he was shot from both sides and above with a forceful spray of water and some sort of noxious cleaning chemicals. He grimaced as he was attacked on all sides by giant spinning blue brushes.

"This never gets any less humiliating," he heard Delphine say somewhere behind him.

Randy was bombarded with a torrent of foamy soap, much of which went directly into his eyes, nose, and mouth.

"Dude, this is so much fun!" Larry shouted from somewhere in the back, and Randy heard Kelli sigh.

There was another blast of water from all sides, and then Randy was thrown to the ground by a hurricane-force shot of hot air.

Finally, he went FWAP FWAP FWAP FWAP FWAP FWAP through several hanging curtains of heavy nylon material.

The moving walkway led Randy through an automatic door and out of the sanitation chamber, and deposited him into what looked for all the world like the waiting room in a doctor's office.

He turned and found the others entering after him—Delphine, then Larry, and, after a delay of several minutes, Kelli.

"Can we do that again?" asked Larry, with a childlike grin on his face.

"*Welcome to PhinCom*," announced a robotic female voice from a speaker mounted near the ceiling. "*Your visit is important to us. Our agents will be with you shortly. In the meantime, please enjoy our selection of easy listening and smooth jazz classics.*"

"Son of a—" started Larry as the music started to play.

"What's the etiquette on continuing to vomit at this point?" asked Randy.

"This part typically only lasts twenty to twenty five minutes," said Delphine.

"So..." said Randy, "I guess these FLIPPER guys get a lot of visitors?"

"No," Delphine said.

"Then...They're just really busy with their intelligence work?" suggested Larry.

"Nope," said Kelli. "Just assholes."

After a good half hour or so of smooth jazz and bickering, a panel opened quite suddenly and noiselessly in one of the walls of the waiting room.

"*FLIPPER will see you now*," said the robotic voice. "*Will you require assistance in locating the council chambers?*"

"We're good," said Kelli. "Ok, boys, follow us."

They stepped through the door into a breathtakingly grandiose hemispherical glass cavern that extended as far as the eye could see. The transparent domed outer walls and ceiling of the chamber were adorned with powerful exterior lighting, revealing a fathomless ocean environment teeming with life of every conceivable shape, color, and form. The interior had the look of an ultramodern airport terminal, all chrome and glass panels, while the floor was a patchwork of concrete, tile, and sunken water features that seemed to connect in a complex series of canals and pools through which swam dolphins, fish, and other varieties of sea life.

Delphine led them through a labyrinth of rooms and corridors, until they came at last to a vast open plain dominated by an enormous stepped pyramid constructed of rectangular grayish-purple stones. A smooth path led to a monumental wooden gate at the front of the pyramid that could easily accommodate any mythological giant.

Delphine stopped at the gate and emitted a series of bizarre chirping noises that sounded roughly like the speech of dolphins, and with a massive grating sound of wood on stone in ancient mechanisms, the door swung inward.

"This is the most amazing place I've ever seen!" Randy whispered to Larry. "I don't even know what to compare it to! It's just—"

"I'm thinking 'Total Recall' meets 'Stargate' meets 'The Abyss.'"

"Uh...ok," said Randy. "Thanks for ruining the moment. Dick."

The giant gate opened into a large, dark chamber that appeared to extend the full length of the inside of the pyramid. They saw featureless gray stone walls and flooring for as far as the external light could penetrate.

Delphine stepped in first and walked toward the shadowy depths of the room. The others hesitated, then quickly began to follow so as not to lose sight of their guide. Once everyone was beyond the threshold, the stone gate began to close behind them, guided by some unknown mechanism. As it finally closed with a heavy thud, they were left in pitch blackness.

Randy had gone to a sensory deprivation tank place once, some years back, hoping to find himself in the complete lack of external stimuli. What he found instead were mild boredom, an inability to shut off his overactive mind, and greater than usual difficulty in ignoring his chronic digestive issues.

His nervousness now was bringing his attention back to his intestinal difficulties, and he noticed a similar lack of stimuli, save for the hard stones beneath the worn tread of his shoes, and the sound of gentle waves breaking against a rocky shore.

"Greetings, topsiders," said a loud, squeaky voice that echoed throughout the dark, massive chamber. *"Wet enough for you out there? I smell that our sanitation procedures have yet to be perfected."*

"Here we go," muttered Delphine, with a clearly audible sigh.

23. BABBLE AND FISH

Kelli was the first to speak. "Greetings, oh illustrious council of—"

"*Oh, cut the shit!*" said the squeaky dolphin voice. "*Why are you here? And who are these—Wait, did you bring the red herrings?*"

"The…" Kelli paused, then cleared her throat loudly. "As I told you before, the fish guy who we go to for our usual peace offerings had a distribution delay, and it became a whole thing…we'll get you the herrings next time, I promise."

"*You'll—Wait, what? I was just asking if OHHHHH, right. Shit. That's, uh…really disappointing because we dolphins just really love to eat herrings! Just can't get me enough of those herrings, boy howdy!*"

"Did he just say 'boy howdy?'" asked Larry, in his closest approximation of a whisper.

"I think so," Randy whispered. "And anyway, how are these dolphins even speaking English?"

"I don't know, it's probably like the old Universal Translator trope from all the bad sci-fi movies or something."

"*The acoustics in this chamber, coupled with our superior senses, allow us to hear everything that you say,*" said the dolphin voice, "*And indeed, with our advanced intellects we have managed to perfect the universal translation device.*"

"Ooh, is it a fish?" asked Randy.

"*A fish? Why on Gaia's blue earth would a translation device be a fish? It's an artificial intelligence program, you speciesist nitwits!*"

"Hey," said Larry, "So, like, is it just you here? I thought this was supposed to be a council or something."

"*Do not attempt to understand FLIPPER with your feeble human brains. FLIPPER speaks in one voice, and behind this voice are forces that you could not hope to comprehend if—*"

"So you're like the Borg?" asked Larry.

"*We do not know your ridiculous topsider references.*"

"Would you say that resisting you is futile?" asked Randy.

"*Yes, obviously. Why do you ask?*"

"Yep, Borg," said Larry. "Sweet!"

Delphine sighed. "So we wanted to—"

"*And you! Compromising the security of our base by bringing The One to us?*"

"We've followed protocol to the letter," replied Kelli.

"*Ooh, well la-di-da, you've followed a security protocol developed by a land-based mutant tribe of hairless monkeys? That makes us feel better! And for what? For a measly little...for...a...a...wait, what is it you came here for, again?*"

"That's what I was trying to tell you."

"*Oh, right. fine. Well, what's taking you so long, then? Spit it out already!*"

"Paul the Octopus may be alive."

There was a pause.

"*Huh. Well that's unfortunate.*"

"Yes. We couldn't tell you over the standard communications channels because we are beginning to fear they've been compromised," Kelli added.

"*Well, nevermind. With this new information our operatives can quickly hunt down Paul and remove him from the picture. Consider it done. However, something else has emerged from our latest intelligence.*"

"Which is?" Delphine asked.

"*It seems that in the final filing of the paperwork, our tentacled friends have not submitted their ISIS application on behalf of the order Octopoda.*"

"That doesn't make sense," Kelli interjected. "Then how did they file it?"

"They filed as the class Cephalopoda."

Pause.

"But..." said Delphine.

Longer pause.

"That would mean..." said Kelli.

"Yes," the dolphin voice said. *"The Kraken."*

"The Kraken?" Larry laughed. "What, like in 'Pirates of the Caribbean?' Or 'Clash of the Titans?'"

"Ooh! Or 'Lord of the Rings!'" added Randy.

"No, that's a Watcher in the Water," Larry corrected. "They never actually call that one a kraken."

"Sure, but in David Day's 'Tolkien Bestiary' he—"

Kelli cleared her throat pointedly. "Guys? Focus?"

"Right," said Randy. "You were saying?"

"Yes," said Kelli. "As you know, all octopuses are cephalopods, but not all cephalopods are octopuses."

"Uh, yeah. Totally," said Larry, his bewildered expression thankfully hidden by the darkness of the chamber.

"The Kraken," Kelli said, "is an ancient cephalopod intelligence that uses a power similar to standard Octopossession. But where standard Octopossession can only invade the more pliable and somewhat weaker minds of humans, the Kraken developed the ability to possess the minds of other cephalopods. It can control numerous minds at the same time, and by passing itself through ever younger cephalopod hosts, it has managed to continually propagate and evolve its consciousness continuum for many thousands, if not millions, of years."

There was silence as everyone paused to ponder the implications of this new development.

"So, like, this Kraken guy is pretty smart, then?" asked Larry.

"So this Kraken guy is pretty smart, then?" mimicked FLIPPER.

"Oh, shove it up your blowhole!" said Larry.

"If the Kraken is present at The Reckoning," said Delphine, "then all hope for humankind is lost."

"Well that's unfortunate," said Randy.

"'*The Reckoning?*'" asked FLIPPER. "*You humans are always trying to sound so sophisticated. Didn't you tell them the real name?*"

"We...don't like the real name," said Delphine.

"Dude, what's the real name?" asked Larry.

"*Cosmic IDOL!*"

"Thanks," said Kelli. "Yes, ISIS calls their admissions process the Cosmic Intelligence Diagnostic for Organic Lifeforms. Cosmic IDOL. But the stupid octopuses went and ruined that name too!"

"What are you talking about?" said Larry. "Cosmic IDOL sounds way cooler than The Reckoning!"

"Are you kidding?" said Randy. "The Reckoning sounds like a Nine Inch Nails album or something."

"Huh," said Larry. "I was thinking maybe Busta Rhymes. Ooh, hey, maybe a Nine Inch Nails and Busta collabo?"

"That would be amazing!" said Randy.

"Uh...guys?" said Kelli. "Your entire species is about to become extinct if we don't figure something out here."

"You mean *our* entire species," corrected Randy.

"Right, sure. Our entire species is about to become extinct if we don't figure something out here."

"*Oh, so you're still pretending to be human? How cute.*"

"Wait, what?" asked Randy.

"People! Can we please. Just. Focus!" Kelli shouted.

"Look," said Delphine. "Clearly the only way out of this is to find The Kraken, and to keep it the hell away from...Cosmic IDOL. So."

She paused for dramatic effect.

"Let's get Kraken."

◆ ◆ ◆

"Guys? I said 'Let's get Kraken.'" repeated Delphine.

"Yeah, we heard you," said Kelli. "And did you just pause for dramatic effect?"

"No! Nobody does that. I just thought, you know, *Kraken*, like—"

"No, yeah, we got it," said Randy.

"*What do you want here, a trophy?*"

"Whatever," said Delphine. "I hate you guys."

"So," said Larry. "How do we find The Kraken?"

"*You do not find The Kraken,*" said FLIPPER ominously. "*The Kraken finds you.*"

"Oh," said Larry. "Well, then. That sounds more convenient anyway, I guess."

"*The Kraken will have already discovered all of your secrets and infiltrated your organization at the deepest levels. Its hosts may be all around you as we speak. We are investigating as quickly as we can, but you must return to your Cosmic IDOL preparations with extreme caution. Trust nobody!*"

"I feel like we hear that a lot," said Randy.

"Are we supposed to be preparing?" asked Larry. "Because we talked about—"

BWAA! BWAA! BWAA! BWAA!

"The hell is that?" asked Randy.

BWAA! BWAA! BWAA! BWAA!

"*That would be the PhinCom highest security threat level alarm. Thanks a lot, topsiders. We're under attack.*"

BWAA! BWAA! BWAA! BWAA!

"We...followed protocol," Kelli muttered weakly.

BWAA! BWAA! BWAA! BWAA!

"*Alarms off!*" said FLIPPER. "*Activate all exterior environmental monitors, maximum radius.*"

A sprawling, multicolored holographic image appeared suddenly in the darkness in front of them. It was some sort of complex data visualization that Randy and Larry couldn't make any sense of, and it seemed to throb and pulsate as though alive.

"It appears that there is a massive attack force converging on us from all directions."

"But why? Why would they be attacking you now?" asked Kelli. "Your location has hardly been a secret."

"Because you brought these idiots here! Duh!"

"Did he just say 'Duh?'" asked Randy.

"Let's see now, it appears we have sharks, octopuses, giant squids, eels, jellyfish, various large fish species..."

"Who cares?" said Delphine. "Those things can't even begin to breach your outermost defenses."

"And something bigger."

There was a long silence as they continued to watch the strange holograph change and evolve.

"It isn't possible."

"No," said Kelli. "It can't be. There must be some other—"

"There is only one entity this massive and this eldritch in all the depths of the oceans."

"Are...are you as lost as I am?" whispered Randy.

"Hundred percent," said Larry.

"That dark patchy section over there does look pretty eldritch," said Delphine.

"Why do they keep saying 'eldritch?'" whispered Larry.

"The data is clear. This can mean only one thing."

"But. But they wouldn't," said Kelli.

"They have."

"Have...?" asked Larry.

"They have freed Cthulhu."

"Well that's unfortunate," said Delphine.

24. THE OLD GODS

"Uh...guys?" said Larry. "What's a Cthulhu?"

"We're talking Cthulhu, like that gigantic evil humanoid octopus monster thing that H.P. Lovecraft made up?" asked Randy.

"Yeah, about that," replied Kelli. "He didn't. It's an actual thing."

"Huh," said Randy. "Well then, that really is unfortunate."

"So you've read about this guy?" Larry asked. "And you'd say he's pretty eldritch?"

"Oh, yeah," agreed Randy. "Cthulhu is eldritch as fuck."

"Oh, ok," said Larry. "And just one more thing. What's eldritch?"

"Just, like, weird and bad," said Randy.

"Ah. And you guys couldn't just say weird and bad?"

"With Cthulhu you have to say 'eldritch,'" said Randy. "It's just a thing. But hey, isn't Cthulhu supposed to be imprisoned for all time in the sunken lost city of R'lyeh?"

"Supposed to be, yes," said Kelli. "That's kind of the problem we're facing here."

"Ah, ok, cool," said Larry. "Well then I think I'm caught up. Carry on."

"Well," said Kelli. "This is significantly worse than The Kraken. With Cthulhu on the loose, your species won't even survive long enough to make it to The Reckoning and worry about The Kraken beating you."

"Yeah, so about all of this 'your species' business..." Randy started.

"*There is one way,*" interrupted FLIPPER.

"What are you talking about?" asked Kelli.

"*Unleashing Cthulhu is a clear violation of the ancient treaties,*" FLIPPER continued. "*As such, we are now free of their binding power.*"

"And?" asked Delphine. "What exactly are you suggesting?"

"*The answer is clear. We release Yahweh.*"

There was a pause.

"Ok," said Larry, "I was definitely not caught up. What?"

"Yahweh, like...God?" asked Randy.

"One of them, yes," said Kelli.

"Again...what?" asked Larry.

"It's a long story," said Kelli. "ISIS assigns each candidate species one or more GODs, or General Operational Directors, to assist with the candidacy process. Cthulhu used to be the GOD of the octopuses, and Yahweh was the primary GOD of the humans. Others called him Zeus, Brahman...you know. Anyway, they both caused a bit too much trouble on the job, so Cthulhu was locked up in the lost city of R'lyeh, and Yahweh was and still is locked up in a secret chamber underneath the Vatican. What do you think all those Swiss Guards are there for?"

"To...protect the Pope?" said Randy.

"Right," Delphine laughed.

"So wait," said Larry. "If Yahweh's locked up, then who is GOD right now?"

"*That would be your friend Kali, here,*" said FLIPPER.

All eyes turned to Kelli.

"Kali?" asked Randy. "Like from the Vedas and Puranas?"

"Kali?" asked Larry. "Like from 'Indiana Jones and the Temple of Doom?'"

"No!" said Kelli. "Not like from 'Indiana Jones and—' Ok fine, a little bit like from 'Indiana Jones and the Temple of Doom.' But I never asked those guys to do all that gross heart stuff! That was all them."

"Sweet!" said Larry. "Dude, Randy. You're dating an angry

goddess."

"I'm not—We're not even—She's not an angry goddess!" cried Randy.

"I'm starting to be!" said Kelli. "And you, FLIPPER. I may be the candidacy representative to the humans, but you know that I still work for ISIS. And as such you know that I can't allow you to free Yahweh when he has been lawfully incarcerated under the relevant intergalactic legal code."

"You know it's the only way, Kali. Without Yahweh free to maintain a balance of power, Cthulhu will have destroyed mankind within hours!"

"Hey you guys," Larry interrupted. "You remember a few minutes ago when we were all worried about Paul the Octopus? I miss that."

"Yeah, that did escalate surprisingly quickly," Randy agreed.

"And you don't have to allow it," FLIPPER continued. *"You just have to look the other way while we get it done."*

"I can't, FLIPPER," she repeated.

"You know that communications at PhinCom core are completely secured," continued FLIPPER. *"Not even ISIS can tap into this conversation right now. Maybe you're feeling a bit tired. Maybe you go have a few drinks after this and just sort of...forget that we had this conversation."*

"I...but..." stuttered Kelli.

"It is the only way, Kali."

"Goddamn it," Kelli sighed. "I hate you guys."

"So, uhm...what are we doing about Cthulhu?" asked Larry.

"We're releasing Yahweh."

"Yeah, no, that's cool," said Larry. "Yay, Yahweh! I'm a big fan, trust me. But I mean like right now. Because it looks like the big eldritch part of that holograph thingie keeps creeping closer."

"*Oh, right. That. We can utilize our standard escape procedure, which will briefly transport the entire PhinCom base into an alternate dimension.*"

"Awesome!" said Larry.

"*However, without sufficient preparation, the strange geometries of that place would render your weak human brains hopelessly and irreparably insane within moments.*"

"Somewhat less awesome," said Randy.

"*Also, the attackers are looking for you two, and the alternate dimension trick will only hold them off briefly. We will use it as a diversionary tactic and for our own getaway, while having you escape undetected in a different way.*"

"Which is?" Larry asked.

"*We shall commence...the Jonah Protocol.*"

There was a pause.

"Well that's unfortunate," said Delphine.

"The Jonah Protocol," repeated Randy. "Is...is that anything like what it sounds like?"

"It's exactly like what it sounds like," said Delphine.

"Wait, what does it sound like?" asked Larry.

"Well," said Randy. "You know how you say you try to base your entire life on The Bible?"

"Yeah."

"And have you ever tried reading it?" asked Randy.

"Why would I do that?"

"Ok. So, Jonah was a guy who got swallowed by a whale and lived in its stomach for three days before being vomited out on the shore."

"Ew," said Larry. "And anyway that's not from The Bible, that's from 'Pinocchio.'"

"Ah, right," said Randy. "I knew it was one of those two."

"Technically the original Hebrew doesn't specify a

whale," said Delphine. "It just says a big fish."

"So...we're not going in the stomach of a whale?" asked Randy.

"No, yeah, you are," she said. "They use a whale here."

"Then why did you bring it up?!"

"There are whales all around these waters," explained FLIP-PER, *"And they will all be fleeing from Cthulhu and the incoming invasion force. Nobody will look twice at Blubber."*

"Blubber?" asked Randy.

"Yes. Blubber is the most experienced and trustworthy member of our sperm whale escape squad."

Larry snickered.

"Let it go, Larry," whispered Randy. "Anyway, sperm whales are the only whales with throats wide enough to swallow an adult human."

Larry snickered again. "Dude. Why do you even know that?"

"I have no idea," whispered Randy.

"We can still hear you guys, by the way," said FLIPPER.

"We'll have Blubber deposit you somewhere safe," said Kelli, "and we'll arrange for your immediate pickup. In the meantime, we've got some advanced deep-sea diving suits in the supersonic sub, you can take those for the ride. They'll take care of temperature control, bathroom needs, not being instantly killed by digestive juices or depth pressure, and so forth. It'll still be a bit claustrophobic, but you should make it out alive."

"Everybody brace yourselves, the advance attack force is about to reach the base," warned FLIPPER.

There was a loud crash, and the floor of the chamber began to shake and sway violently.

"Quick! While there is still time! Escort these two morons to the sperm swallowing pool!"

"Should I... Should I let that one go, too?" Larry asked in near hysterics.

"Probably," whispered Randy, before the two of them

broke out into raucous, uncontrollable laughter.

25. THE JONAH BROTHERS

"Well, this is awkward," said Randy.

"I really thought there'd be more room than this inside a whale's stomach," said Larry.

"And this is after they've converted the typical four-chambered stomach into a single escape pod."

"Well, it's sure not a very comfortable escape pod," said Larry.

"It'd be cozier if your ass wasn't right in my face," said Randy. "Can you move at all?"

"Not really. Can you?"

"No," Randy sighed.

"These diving suits are pretty sweet, though," said Larry. "Hey, can we really just pee in these things and it takes care of it?"

"Supposedly. You can try first."

"Maybe later," said Larry. "Well, they said we'd probably have a day or so to kill in here. What should we do?"

"I think our choices are fairly limited."

"Here. I spy with my little eye...something that starts with 'D.'"

"Darkness," said Randy. "Uhm...I spy with my little eye-...uhm...yeah, I think we've pretty much exhausted this game."

"As long as they're converting these whales' stomachs, why don't they add some lighting or something?" asked Larry.

"You want to see the inside of a whale's stomach?"

"Good point."

◆ ◆ ◆

"Hey, Randy. You awake?"

"Grbbhlfpppph. Uhm. What?"

"Are you awake?" Larry repeated.

"I am now. What time is it?"

"How do I know what time it is? We're inside a whale."

"Oh, right," said Randy. "Shit. Why'd you wake me up, man? I'm hungry and there's nothing to eat here."

"Didn't you listen to the onboarding lecture?" asked Larry. "This straw thingie by your mouth is connected to a tank of protein gunk or something."

"I don't think I'm that hungry yet," said Randy.

"Tell me about it," said Larry. "I almost tried it. But yeah, I'm pretty hungry and extremely bored."

"So go to sleep."

"I tried," said Larry, "but I can't stop thinking."

"That's unusual," said Randy. "What are you thinking about?"

"Oh, just this whole Cosmic IDOL competition, and all that. And also Kelli. Like, if she's really some kind of alien goddess or something, do you think she'll still go out with you?"

"Yeah, I'm thinking probably no."

"Maybe," said Larry. "But hey, if she did, do you think she has, you know…normal parts?"

"So you were lying awake inside this whale wondering if the woman I have a crush on is anatomically correct?"

"Yes."

"Huh," said Randy. "Thanks, I guess. You're a good friend. Anyway, I have no idea. I mean, what is she, anyway? Some kind of alien species that just looks like humans? Or some kind of magical shapeshifter? Or is she just an alien intelligence invading a human body, like the octopuses do? Who even knows."

"Oh well," said Larry. "Whatever she is, she still seems pretty cool. She has a decent sense of humor for an alien. Plus, I didn't want to kill your mojo before when we were trying to ask her out, but she's crazy hot."

"Yeah," said Randy. "I guess she is. But like you said—"

PSSHHHHZZZ!

"What was that?" asked Larry.

"I don't—"

PSSHHHHZZZ!

"That's weird, I wonder—"

PSSHHHHZZZ! ATTENTION ORB AGENTS, HQ HAS ISSUED A CODE ORANGE TO ALL AVAILABLE PERSONNEL AT OR ABOVE CLEARANCE LEVEL C.

"It seems to be coming from the suits," said Randy. "Is that normal?"

"I don't know," said Larry. "Are we at or above Clearance Level C?"

"I feel like we'd know that sort of thing if we were," said Randy. "These suits were in Kelli and Delphine's sub. It must be a transmission meant for them! Should we, like, try not to listen or something?"

PSSHHHHZZZ! CODE ORANGE INFORMATION TO FOLLOW. SUBJECTS ROBO AND ROBEY HAVE BEEN CAPTURED BY THE ENEMY. RECOVERY NOT EXPECTED IN TIME FOR IDOL. ALTERNATE POSSIBLE SUBJECTS ALL CAPTIVE. EFFECTIVE IMMEDIATELY, RED HERRING SUBJECTS GOOFY AND DOPEY ARE OFFICIALLY THE ONE. AGENTS ARE DIRECTED TO PROCEED ACCORDINGLY."

There was an awkward silence.

"Well, that was weird," said Randy.

"Red herrings…" said Larry. "Didn't FLIPPER say something about eating red herrings?"

"He asked if Kelli and Delphine had brought the red herrings. You know, it's funny, in literature a 'red herring' is something that's supposed to mislead or trick you."

"So someone got captured," said Larry. "And everyone

124

else is already captured…and now some two guys are The One."

"The only guys not captured. But…"

"We haven't been captured," said Larry.

"Holy shit!" cried Randy. "We're Goofy and Dopey!"

"But that would mean—"

"We weren't really The One at all! We were the red herrings!"

"Son of a bitch!" said Larry. "So they've just been parading us around like a couple of undercover celebrities to…to…"

"To get us captured by the octopuses, so they would think they had The One, and let their guard down leading up to the Cosmic IDOL competition!"

"See?" said Larry. "What did I tell you? That bastard Hachi had no intention of rescuing us at all! He was going to let us rot in that cell until after IDOL!"

"Meanwhile," said Randy, "some dudes called Robo and Robey would show up unharmed, and compete on behalf of the human race!"

"And obviously do a lot better than us, because they're probably smart!" added Larry.

"Damn it, that's actually a pretty good plan," said Randy.

"I knew it was weird that they kept telling us we didn't need to study or prepare for Cosmic IDOL in any way," said Larry.

"Goddamn it," said Randy.

"Hey, remember a few minutes ago when we thought your girlfriend was a pretty cool space alien?" said Larry. "I miss that."

PSSHHHHZZZ!

"Great, now what?" asked Randy.

PSSHHHHZZZ! Calling Randy and Larry. Kelli here, with Delphine. Can you hear us?

"Oh hello, Ladies," Larry said pointedly. "So nice to hear from you."

PSSHHHHZZZ! Thank you, you too. Listen. There's been a slight change of plans. We're going to have Blubber drop you off at a sort of training facility, where you can do just a little bit of prep work to sharpen you up for Cosmic IDOL.

"Oh?" asked Larry. "Interesting. I thought you said that sort of thing wasn't necessary."

"Oh, and by the way," said Randy. "GOOFY AND DOPEY?!"

PSSHHHHZZZ!

Silence.

PSSHHHHZZZ!

Silence.

PSSHHHHZZZ! Shit. You guys heard all that?

"Yes we heard all that!" yelled Larry. "What the hell, man?"

"You were just using us as octopus bait?" asked Randy.

PSSHHHHZZZ! Well I wouldn't put it like that...

"So you weren't just using us as octopus bait?" asked Larry.

PSSHHHHZZZ! Oh, no, we totally were, I just wouldn't put it like that. Look, guys, you have to look at the big picture. The entire fate of mankind is in our hands here!

"I don't care if the fate of the universe is in your hands!" Larry said. "That was a dick move!"

PSSHHHHZZZ! Yeah, well. Sorry. Now we need to—

"So who are Robo and Robey?" asked Randy.

PSSHHHHZZZ! Right. That would be Stephen Hawking and His Holiness the Dalai Lama.

"Oh, yeah?!" shouted Larry. "Well...well...Fine! Damn it. Those guys would totally be way better at this than us."

"I mean, obviously," said Randy.

"Hold on," said Larry. "What about that rule where The One can't be too smart? You know, that whole thing about the deviated septum..."

"Could you mean standard deviation?" Randy interrupted.

"I could mean standard deviation!" Larry cried. "See? Stephen Hawking would have known that!"

"I knew that," said Randy. "Look, dude. Don't you get it?

It's not a real rule! They just made that shit up to explain how a couple of dumbasses like us could be The One!"

"Ohhhh," said Larry. "So they just said The One couldn't be too smart because they wanted us to think we were The One, and they knew that we weren't too smart?"

"Uh huh," said Randy. "And they knew that we knew that we weren't too smart."

"Huh. That's pretty smart."

"Yeah," said Randy. "But wait. Didn't Stephen Hawking die?"

PSSHHHHZZZ! Technically, yes. Which was a bit of a problem for our planning. Luckily it turned out that shortly before his death, he had managed to upload his full consciousness matrix into an advanced neural network that he had built within the framework of his chair.

"Oh yeah?!" shouted Randy. "Well that's...that's... Damn it. That's really awesome. I was really beginning to question whether that sort of thing would ever be possible, what with the 'hard problem of consciousness' in neuroscience and all. Wow, I have to say, that really—"

"Uh, dude? Can we focus?" asked Larry.

"Right," said Randy. "Yes. Still angry. So...why should we help you now?"

PSSHHHHZZZ! Mostly because with everyone else captured, you're now the last hope for mankind.

"Yeah, well..." Larry grumbled. "I don't really like them that much anyway."

"Me neither," agreed Randy. "Especially that Craig Kim."

"Not to mention Shia LaBeouf!" Larry added.

"Oh, don't even get me started on—"

PSSHHHHZZZ! Fine. Look. Randy, if you guys do this prep work and come compete in Cosmic IDOL for us, I'll go on a date with you.

Randy and Larry paused and looked at each other. At least that's how they imagined it, although in reality they couldn't look at anything in the absolute blackness and Larry's butt was still in Randy's face.

"What's the point?" Randy asked. "You don't even like me. You sold me out!"

PSSHHHHZZZ! I like you Randy, I really do. I just have a job to do, and I'm...really dedicated to my career.

"You'll go on a date with me, a real date, before the entire human species is obliterated?"

PSSHHHHZZZ! Yes! I mean no, the human species isn't going to be obliterated. You guys can still win this. Cephalopods are smart in a certain kind of way, but I don't think they have the kind of intelligence that ISIS is looking for. But humans...you're what we want! Even with a couple of normal guys like yourselves, I'm confident that the panel will see that! Just do the training, show up, and you'll see.

"Ok," said Randy. "But if mankind is to be destroyed, and you're aware of it, our date comes before that."

PSSHHHHZZZ! Ok. Deal.

"Alright, fine," said Larry. "So. What do we do now?"

PSSHHHHZZZ! Blubber is going to transport you to a special training center. You'll have one full day to learn as much as you can from the available resources, at which point you will be picked up by one of our agents and transported to the secret location of the Cosmic IDOL competition.

"Fine," said Randy. "So, how do we know what to learn at this training center? What do we focus on?"

PSSHHHHZZZ! I don't know. Whatever kinds of things you think would best demonstrate human intelligence to a panel of alien judges. Think about what kinds of things Stephen Hawking and The Dalai Lama would know.

"Huh," said Larry. "Ok."

PSSHHHHZZZ! Oh and one thing. You'll need the following password...

26. RAPPER NUI

Randy and Larry found themselves vomited quite suddenly and unceremoniously into a warm, sunny, and actually rather pleasant day at the beach. They couldn't tell how long they had been in the belly of the whale, as they had lost all track of time in the dark, cramped quarters. As they climbed slowly and painfully out of their deep sea gear and dumped it onto the soft white sand, they saw Blubber heading back out into the ocean. They waved goodbye as it sank slowly out of sight.

"Well, that was unpleasant," said Randy. "So. Where do you suppose we are?"

"Based on that giant head on the hill over there," Larry replied, "I'm gonna go with either the Natural History Museum, or..."

Randy looked at him expectantly until it was clear that he wasn't planning to continue because he couldn't remember the name he was looking for. "Rapa Nui?" he suggested.

"What? No," said Larry. "I don't even speak whatever language that was. Help me out, here. I mean the place. You know, with the heads."

"Easter Island," said Randy. "The question is...why?"

"Beats me," said Larry. "But I only see one person around here to ask."

They walked up the gentle grassy slope toward the head, which proved to be about three times their height. They walked around it, looking up in awe and feeling the ancient stone.

"This is pretty awesome," said Randy. "But I really thought we'd be going to Egypt after Kelli said our password was 'Alexandria.'"

"Egypt?" Larry replied. "What's in Egypt? I was just hoping we were gonna be training with a hot chick named Alexandria. Oh well. Hey, wouldn't it be funny if this thing started talking?"

"WHY WOULD IT BE 'FUNNY' IF THIS 'THING' STARTED TALKING?" came a deep, booming voice that shook the ground around them like an earthquake.

"AAAAAAAAAAGGHHH!" replied Randy and Larry.

"Sorry," the statue said, its amorphously featured face now kicking into full animation as it spoke. "I tend to have volume control issues when I haven't spoken for some time. Now, welcome to Rapa Nui. Your password checks out against the latest updates. What can I do for you?"

"AAAAAAAAAAGGHHH!" replied Randy and Larry.

"Yes, you've said," the statue sighed.

"IT'S TALKING!" shouted Larry.

"I could say the same of you," the statue said calmly.

"Well, sure," replied Randy, "but we're supposed to talk."

"And?" asked the enormous statue. "I'm supposed to talk, too. In fact, that's the sole purpose for which I was designed. Whereas you were designed primarily for reproduction. So I should be the one complaining here, when you think about it. Hey, somebody! Why are these breeders talking at me?"

"Well," said Larry, "these breeders are talking at you because we're here for our training. We're The One."

The gigantic statue raised a hint of a stone eyebrow. "You're The One?" it asked.

"Yes, we're The One," said Randy.

"And what happened to Hawking and His Holiness?"

"Captured," said Larry. "Along with all of the backup Ones, apparently."

"Interesting," said the statue. "And you are?"

"A red herring, meant to throw the octopuses off the trail of the real One," said Randy. "Only now everyone else is gone and we're what's left, so we were told to train for Cosmic IDOL."

There were a few moments of silence.

"Huh," said the statue. "Well, that's unfortunate. So what do you want from me?"

"That depends," said Randy. "I mean...what are you? And what is this place?"

"This is Easter Island," said the statue. "The real one, of course. The one that they take all the tourists to is a replica. Wouldn't want any of them accidentally triggering one of us."

"One of what, exactly?" asked Larry.

"I'm a Mo'ai."

"What, like in Gremlins?"

"No," the statue sighed. "That's a mogwai. Mo'ai are the famous Easter Island statues. This entire island is a data center designed on ancient technology, to act as a continuously updated, single-source repository of all human knowledge. The Mo'ai are like interactive terminals for querying the database. You ask, I answer. I can tell you anything you want to know, provided it's something that humans collectively already know or have learned."

"So...you can teach us stuff?" asked Larry.

"In theory, yes," said the statue. "What do you want to know?"

"Do you know who killed Tupac?" Larry asked.

"Yes. But let me rephrase my question. What are you supposed to know?"

"Well, that's just it," said Randy. "We don't really know what it is that we need to know."

There was a brief pause.

"Why are you wasting my time?" asked the statue.

"Look, we're not trying to waste your time," said Larry. "We just need to know everything that Stephen Hawking and the Dalai Lama would know..."

They heard a faint, derisive snort.

"Was that a faint, derisive snort?" asked Randy.

"Yes," said the statue. "Must be volume issues again, as it was meant to be significantly louder. Alright, guys. Just so I know what we're working with here. If they've picked you to be The One, albeit after some hiccups in the process, then may I assume that you're at least...smart?"

"No," said Larry.

"I mean," said Randy, "that's really kind of subj—I mean it's all a matter of—No, not really."

"But seriously," said Larry. "Who did it?"

"You know, I'll miss you people, in a way," said the statue.

"Me and Larry?" Randy asked.

"Humans. I mean, as an automaton I don't have that particular emotion per se, but one does get used to a certain lifestyle. Then again, I never really did like your species very much on the whole."

"You don't like our species?" Larry asked. "What did we do?"

"Well, for starters," said the statue, "you always just come around here and start asking questions without so much as a hello. I mean, would it hurt you to just take a moment for small talk, and maybe even ask how I'm doing?"

"Oh," said Randy. "Huh. Well then, how are you doing?"

"Terrible! For one thing, this is probably the last time that I'll be activated. But hey, maybe that's a good thing. I mean, look around you! Look at this place!"

They did.

"It looks pretty nice to me," said Larry.

"Yeah," said the statue. "And what looks pretty nice about it?"

"The ocean, the—"

"Ah, yes, the ocean," said the statue. "You know, I can tell you anything you ever wanted to know about the ocean. The flora, the fauna, the topography, the chemical composition, you name it. From the broadest knowledge to the minutest detail. But you know what I can't do?"

"What?"

"SEE THE OCEAN!" the statue shouted.

"But it's right over—Ohhhhh..." said Randy.

"Exactly! All of the Mo'ai were built right next to the big, beautiful ocean, facing inland! I've literally never seen the damn thing! Yes, sir, a real class act, your species."

"I mean if you just—" Larry said, turning his head slightly to one side.

"DO I LOOK LIKE I SWIVEL?!"

"No, I suppose not," Randy sighed. "Wait, my pretty-boy friend here is bound to have a mirror."

"A mirror?" Larry laughed. "Dude, we were just vomited out of the belly of a whale, and you think...you think...wait, yeah, no, I actually do have a mirror. But what's your point?"

"Wait for it," Randy said to the statue.

"What?" Larry asked.

"Wait for it," Randy repeated.

"No, I just actually don't know what you're getting at here," said Larry.

"So, you two are The One, you say?" asked the statue.

"Looks that way," Randy confirmed with a sigh.

"Ok now, a little to the left," the statue said. "More. A little more. Now slightly up. Up. There! Stop!"

A silence fell, broken only by the quiet sigh of the salty ocean breeze.

"You can see it alright?" Larry asked.

"I...You guys...I just..."

"Are you crying?" Randy asked.

"No, I'm not crying," the statue replied, through what sounded like soft but steady sobbing. "Technically."

"Look, you guys are alright," said the statue. "And I can see that your species has potential. It's entirely possible that my negative evaluation of your kind has a selection sample bias based on my location and unique job function."

"Thanks," said Randy.

"What?" said Larry.

"He said we're not all dicks," replied Randy.

"Oh. Cool," said Larry. "So you can help us out?"

"Yes," said the statue. "I mean, I kind of had to anyway. It's what I'm programmed for, and you have the password. But I like you guys."

"Ok," said Randy, "So what do we need to know for this Cosmic IDOL competition?"

"Well, nobody knows specifically what occurs during Cosmic IDOL, as ISIS keeps the process a closely guarded secret among member species. The best information available is that it should be something like a job interview. But, you know. For your entire species."

"Great. I hate job interviews," said Randy.

"Oh, uh, me too," said Larry. "Job interviews are the worst."

Randy looked at him suspiciously. "Why'd you say that all weird? Wait, you've been on job interviews before, right?"

"Oh, yeah, totally. All the time. Hate me some job interviews!"

"Dude! You've never been on a job interview!" Randy laughed.

"Fine, you got me," said Larry. "I've just never really had to."

"What? How?"

"Well, you know how I was raised by paranoid anti-government survivalists? So, we lived in a sort of survivalist commune, and I used to work for my dad, scavenging and re-selling military and survival gear. And then...we came into some money, and I guess I haven't really had to worry about that sort of thing since."

"That doesn't even make sense," said Randy. "What money?"

Larry sighed. "Ok, fine. So after Obama took office, my parents became increasingly worried that the government was coming for our guns and our money. What little there was of it, anyway. We used to keep all our cash in a gutted out Bible, because obviously they couldn't trust the banks. My mom said it was blasphemous, but my dad always said that the dirty bastards had never opened a Bible before, and they weren't likely to start with ours."

"Fair enough," said Randy.

"So, one day," said Larry, "My dad goes to one of his meetings, and he comes back all drunk and worked up about how Obama's secret police are on their way right now, and he tells me to get out of there, and take the money and put it somewhere safe."

"Alright," said Randy.

"Well, my friend Unstable Pete had been yapping at me for weeks about some new kind of electronic money that was untraceable, and he was learning all about it so he could stick it to the system, and blah blah blah. So I run to Pete's trailer and hand him the Bible money like ok Pete, make this disappear off the grid."

"So your parents didn't trust the banks," said Randy, "but a guy called Unstable Pete..."

"Oh, they were pissed," said Larry. "I mean, we didn't really know where the money was after that. Hell, I don't think Pete really knew where the money was for a while, it was just out there somewhere in computerland. We had to barter for groceries, other than what we grew in the back, but we made do. Anyway, long story short, my dad's dead of cirrhosis and my mom is richer than J.K. Rowling."

"Wait, what?" said Randy.

"Oh, right," said Larry. "See, Unstable Pete put all of our money into Bitcoin when it was brand new and then progressively cashed out. So...yeah. I haven't really been doing a lot of job interviews I guess."

"But..." Randy muttered, in a daze. "But you live in a shitty apartment in Queens!"

"We try not to attract attention," said Larry.

"Wait, I pay you half the rent on that shitty apartment in Queens!"

"Dude, have you even looked at the market?" Larry laughed. "You barely pay a fifth of the rent on that shitty apartment. Plus I've been donating your checks directly to some charity that provides solar energy to starving third-world kittens or some shit. I figured you'd like that. Anyway, I only put out an ad for a roommate in the first place because I was really lonely. And then out of everybody who came, you seemed like you weren't a dick. Like the statue here said."

"Oh, so you guys can see that I'm still standing here, though?" said the statue. "Because I wasn't really sure."

"Wow, that's…" Randy stuttered. "I don't even know what to say."

"Well," said Larry. "You can start by telling me what happens in one of these job interview dealies."

"I don't know," said Randy. "An interview is mostly just, like, why do you think you're qualified for this job? What are your key strengths and weaknesses? Can you write some SQL Server code on the board to calculate—"

"Yeah," said Larry, "I think that last one may be job-specific…"

27. YOU TELL ME THAT IT'S EVOLUTION

"So, ok," said Larry. "Uhm...statue guy. I'm sorry, do you have an actual name or something?"

"No," said the statue.

"Awesome," said Larry. "Glad I asked. So, what are humans' strengths and weaknesses?"

"Relative to whom?"

"I don't know," Larry said. "Octopuses? Other ISIS members?"

"Well," the statue said, "we don't really know much about other ISIS member species, so we can only speculate in that arena. We have heard rumors that members include some 'First Degree' species of purely evolutionary origin, as humans are to the best of our knowledge, and some 'Nth Degree' or engineered intelligences, such as myself. While lower-stage First Degree intelligences on Earth tend to have more task-oriented minds, higher-stage ones such as humans and octopuses are...a bit of a mess, you might say. I'll ask you a question. Randy, how are you at self control?"

"Oh, well," said Randy, "I practice mindfulness meditation, and—"

"He's awful," said Larry. "He has none. He raids the pantry and the fridge of everything we own except vegetables every night at Netflix o'clock, and he's probably never exercised on purpose in his entire life."

"Thanks, dude," said Randy.

"No matter," said the statue. "So let me ask you, what does it actually mean to lack self control? Does it mean that Randy is trying unsuccessfully to control Randy? In which case, why is Randy trying to do something that Randy doesn't want Randy to do in the first place?"

"Because...part of me wants to?" suggested Randy.

"Which part?" asked the statue. "Your arm? Because then you might be starting to think like an octopus."

"Not that kind of part," said Randy. "Just, like...a voice."

"A will?"

"Sure, I guess."

"But I thought you were one person with one will," said the statue.

"I don't know, it's complicated," said Randy.

"Indeed," said the statue. "You see, the problem isn't that you humans lack willpower, but that you simply have too many different wills in power. Human brains are built on a model that evolutionary psychology calls the modular mind. Basically, various functions that are useful for your physical survival both individually and as a species have evolved as independently operating processes, or modules, inside your brain. They have little interaction between themselves, and are moderated at the top level by what has been optimistically called an executive function, but can be more realistically described as a storytelling ego that rationalizes decisions that have already been made, mostly subconsciously, at any and all levels of the brain. So...if we're trying to determine whether or not you are intelligent, who is even the 'you' in question?"

"So, you're saying that I don't exist?" asked Randy.

"You don't exist as such," said the statue, "but then again, you also don't not exist as such."

"There is no spoon," Larry nodded. "Randy, you're the spoon!"

"We're all the spoon, dumbass," said Randy. "He's talking about our whole species."

"Oh, right," said Larry. "Hey, is all this philosophical stuff why they were sending the Dalai Lama along with Hawking?"

"In part," said the statue. "But you don't have to think of it in such lofty terms. Imagine a Thanksgiving family dinner, where all of the participants see each other rarely, don't especially care for each other, and all have their own entirely different agendas for the evening. Maybe they all drink a bit too much to cope with the uncomfortable situation, personalities rear their ugly heads as the evening marches on, and pretty soon everyone is butting heads as the gathering devolves into utter chaos and everyone regrets that they bothered to come in the first place."

"So...Thanksgiving," said Larry.

"Exactly," said the statue. "Now, think of it this way. You're Thanksgiving. Well, your mind is, anyway."

"Damn it, now I want stuffing," said Randy.

"Ok, this is sounding pretty grim so far," said Larry. "So then, what are our strengths?"

"Well," said the statue. "This modular, distributed nature of your intelligence has several advantages. It seems that these brain modules have a mechanism whereby they can associate themselves to appropriate pre-conscious trigger events. So in emergency scenarios such as fight-or-flight encounters, the subconscious can triage very efficiently to the right modules. In effect 'you' have plenty of survival-focused intelligence and decision-making going on in the background before your conscious mind even becomes aware of a situation."

"So we're good at surviving?" Randy asked.

"Yes," said the statue. "Quite. And in addition, this distributed network and all of its countless connections leads to things like intuition and pattern recognition, which contribute to making you an extraordinarily creative form of intelligence. Thus in every human society, even those struggling to meet their basic needs, you will find stories, song, dance, and art."

"Cool, so we're quick and creative," said Larry. "Then what's the downside of this setup, other than the whole not quite existing deal?"

"How shall I put this in terms you'll understand...?" the statue pondered with a slight sigh. "Y'all cray cray!"

"Now hold up just a minute," said Larry. "How are we crazy? Other than the fact that we're standing here talking to a giant statue."

"Glad you asked," said the statue. "See, your ego, the 'you' that's supposed to be in charge of the whole game, is really not much more than a storyteller. Rather than manage your subconscious processes to ensure behaviors that are in line with your personal beliefs, the ego simply tells stories to rationalize whatever the lower levels of your mind have already decided to do. Its favorite stories, of course, are righteous victim stories."

"What are those?" asked Randy.

"Look at all of the popular fairy tales," said the statue. "Start with a pauper, or an orphan, or a couple of moronic roommates, or some otherwise abused person who is constantly mistreated and taken seriously by no one. Then they find out they're somehow special. It turns out that secretly they've always been royalty, or a wizard, or The One, or whatever. And with this newfound power and prestige, they go on to save the day and maybe have a little laugh at everyone who didn't believe in them."

"So?" asked Larry. "What's the point of that?"

"Well," continued the statue. "Your lower modules, the subconscious animal instincts below the surface, are focused on acquiring all available resources for you at the expense of everyone else. But as an intelligent member of a society, this self-focused attitude causes you considerable cognitive dissonance. How can I place such supreme importance on taking care of myself and perhaps my immediate family, when I'm one person out of eight billion, and a seemingly unremarkable one at that? Shouldn't the collective needs of those around me hold greater weight than my own individual desires, just logically speaking? But then your storytelling ego comes to the rescue and says wait, don't you remember all of our favorite fairy tales?

The hero only seemed unimportant, but was actually the most important person of all! You're just misunderstood, mistreated, underestimated. Deep down there is a secret inside of you, and it makes you the most important person in the whole wide world! And if those other people don't recognize that, and instead act as though they're somehow important and treat you like some regular schlub, well then it's on you to go ahead and take everything that is rightfully yours."

"So everyone fends for himself, and everyone has a satisfactory excuse for it," said Randy.

"Satisfactory to precisely no one except his or her own subconscious, but yes," said the giant statue.

"Wow," said Larry, "So you're talking about stories like King Arthur, Harry Potter, The Princess Diaries…"

"Jesus Christ!" interrupted Randy.

"Well that's a bit offensive," said Larry. "I mean for starters—"

"No!" cried Randy, pointing in the direction of the ocean nearby. "Look!"

"Jesus Christ!" cried Larry, after turning to look. "Hey, uh, Statue Guy, do you normally have octopuses around here?"

"Sure," said the statue, "There's even a native species, the Octopus Rapanui. And you can find octopus petroglyphs nearby representing the—"

"I mean like thousands of them," Larry clarified. "Crawling up onto the beach and coming in our general direction."

"No, that's a new one," the statue said.

"Wait," said Randy, "what's going on with the water over there? Why's it all dark and moving like OH MY GOD HOLY SHIT ARE YOU SEEING THIS LARRY?"

Larry stood frozen, staring ahead as the gargantuan figure arose out of the water like some hideous demon from the darkest pits of hell. It had an anthropoid form composed all of gray, slimy scales, with two enormous leathery wings, and its face was a monstrous snarl of fangs and tentacles, with two glowing red eyes that seemed to stare into the depths of his very soul. It stood at least two or three times the height of any building back home in New York City.

"Dude," said Larry in a low voice. "What's with the giant Predator-looking thingie?"

"Let me guess," said the statue, facing inland as always. "Cthulhu's behind me now, right?"

"Yes," whimpered Randy.

"Huh," said Larry. "Well, you were right about one thing. He is pretty eldritch."

"Technically, though," said Randy, "It's pronounced 'Khlûl'-hoo.' According to H.P. Lovecraft himself. I would've thought you'd know that, statue, seeing as how you're a repository of all human knowledge."

"Oh, I knew that," said the statue. "I just didn't want to sound like a ginormous douche."

"KHLÛL-HOO!" came a great voice suddenly from the other direction, and they all turned to look.

"Whoa," said Larry. "Who is that enormous, bearded old dude with the white robe?"

"That'll be Yahweh," said the statue, looking up at the deity in question, who was quickly approaching from the inland side. "Oh, hey, look at that. I'm facing the right way for once!"

"Wait," said Larry. "Is this about to turn into one of those Godzilla vs. The Giant Whatever kind of situations?"

"It appears highly likely," said the statue. "And you two are standing directly in the center of it. Welp, guess y'all are pretty fucked."

"Us?" asked Larry. "What about you?"

"What do I care?" asked the statue. "I'm just a non-sentient automaton."

"Ah," said Larry. "No ghost in the shell."

"Hey, not bad," said Randy. "But it's 'machine.' Wait, so do we actually have a ghost in the machine?"

"Beats me," said the statue. "Ask that guy."

And if the statue could point, it would have pointed at

the gargantuan, quickly approaching figure of Yahweh, who was now marching steadily across the island toward Cthulhu.

"Also, you should probably run," added the statue.

"Run where?" Randy shouted, looking around frantically.

"Good point," said the statue.

Suddenly there was a swoosh of wind and a loud, grating metallic noise, and something that looked for all the world like a flying saucer from a bad 1950s science fiction film appeared in the sky above them! Two beams of blue light shot out of it directly at Randy and Larry, and before they could say a word, they began ascending quickly toward the mysterious craft.

"You lucky bastards," said the statue.

28. STUFF AND MACHINES

The overwhelming sensation of motion stopped, leaving a confused and disoriented Randy and Larry looking around for answers as their eyes recovered from the blinding blue light, and several humanoid figures began to resolve around them.

"DORIS EX MACHINA, BITCHES!" shouted Doris, the adorable old Executive Admin from Randy's New York office.

"Ow!" said Kelli. "You don't have to shout in my ear, Doris, they're right there."

"It was a heroic one-liner," replied Doris. "It requires a certain oomph."

"What?" asked Larry. "Who is Doris and what's all this about her ex?"

"Well, if you were in your writing class this week on Lazy Plotting, you'd know all about it," laughed Delphine. "How did it work again, Kelli?"

"Oh, see," said Randy, "'Deus ex machina' or 'god from the machine' is a plot device that—"

"Did you seriously just jump in to humansplain about gods showing up in machines right now?" asked Kelli.

"Wait," said Randy. "Delphine is still human, right? So technically I was just mansplaining."

"So which one was that, just now?" asked Larry.

"Er...probably both."

"Anyway," said Larry, "why does everything seem to be

happening in or around machines today? Ghosts, gods...it's too many machines! And also, what the hell is even going on?"

"No idea," said Randy.

"Gingerdoodle?" asked Doris.

"Hell, yes!" said Randy. "Larry, try one of these. Trust me."

"Whatever," said Larry. "Look, I want to start hearing some...some...Ok, seriously, what is in this cookie? It's incredible!"

"Right?" said Randy.

"Sorry for the close call there, boys," said Kelli. "We were trying to let you finish your training for Cosmic IDOL, but those big oafs out there got in the way. Hope you at least got to learn a few useful things from our island friends?"

"Well, sure," said Randy, "I mean it's hard to put into words exactly, but I would venture to say that we had a fairly meaningful exchange of—"

"Nothing at all," said Larry. "We're all screwed. Mankind is doomed."

"Yeah, what he said," agreed Randy.

"I'll take another one of those cookies, though!" Larry added. "So hey, what's with this sweet ride? Is this, like, an actual UFO?"

"Oh, not at all," said Doris, who was seated in what appeared to be the pilot's seat, surrounded by a swiveling three-dimensional array of knobs and buttons. "A UFO would be unidentified. This here is an Identified Flying Object. We know exactly what it is. Well, more or less."

"What do you mean, more or less?" asked Randy.

"See," said Doris, "we captured and reverse-engineered this model back in the late '50s."

"Captured and reverse-engineered?" laughed Kelli. "It's hardly like you've built one. You picked it up off the ground, dusted it off, and pushed a lot of buttons until you figured out how it works. Reverse-engineered!"

"Well to be fair, we did come in one morning to find several of the engineers from the initial investigation team turned inside-out," said Doris.

"Right, that was rather unfortunate," said Kelli. "When they called me in that morning and I saw the mess, I was half convinced that you all were back to offering me human sacrifices."

"And then we got the test flights going, and the same thing started happening to all those cows in remote fields," said Doris. "You know, I still can't figure out why the Atlanteans had to put the radial tractor beam switch on the same joystick as the vertical takeoff thrusters. It practically presses itself on the way up, and then you know you're gonna hear about it in the papers the next day."

"The...Atlanteans?" asked Larry.

"Bunch of Neanderthals," said Doris.

"Which we'll get to," said Delphine. "But for the moment we should be focused on getting these two to Cosmic IDOL."

"And that's where, exactly?" asked Randy.

"Switzerland...more or less," said Kelli. "But we can't just fly this thing right into Swiss airspace, because Bad ORB and The Kraken will be watching too closely. So we're going to use a safehouse in France near the border for the night."

"What, The Chateau?" asked Doris. "Good luck getting any sleep there!"

"Why?" laughed Randy. "Is The Chateau haunted or something?"

"Something like that," said Delphine.

"There's nothing wrong with The Chateau," said Kelli. "We're going to drop you off there, they'll put you up for the night, and then you'll be contacted in the morning by one of our agents, who will guide you discreetly across the border into Switzerland on foot so as to avoid detection."

"Ooh, like the Fellowship of the Ring!" said Larry.

"Uh...sure, I guess," said Kelli.

"Except The Kraken found them," Randy pointed out.

"I told you, that was a Watcher in the Water!" cried Larry. "David Day has no authori—"

"Er, boys?" interrupted Delphine.

"Oh, right. Real life," said Larry. "Ok, so you're flying us to some house in France, then?"

"Yep," said Doris. "We're just above the grounds right now."

"What?" asked Randy. "You picked us up on Easter Island like two minutes ago."

"Yeah, sorry," Doris replied. "This model's a bit more sluggish than the more recent ones. But it gets the job done in a bind. Welp, here you are, then. Le Château de Voltaire."

29. ÉCRASEZ L'INFÂME!

"Voltaire, like the goth singer?" asked Larry.

"Voltaire, like the philosopher?" asked Randy.

"No, and...yes, if you want to call him that," replied Kelli.

"Why wouldn't we want to—"

"Oops, look at the time, gotta run," said Doris.

There was a sudden blur of blue light that left Randy and Larry momentarily blinded.

"Ow!" said Randy. "I can't see anything and my ass hurts. Does your ass hurt?"

"Yeah," said Larry. "I think they beamed us down. Kinda hard."

As their vision slowly came back, they found themselves in the woods. The trees and foliage were somewhat sparse, allowing the waning sun to penetrate sufficiently to illuminate a simple dirt walking trail. Silently they took to the trail, and went in the direction where the light seemed to increase. A short stroll brought them to the edge of the wood.

"Holy crap," said Larry, his gaze focused a short distance directly ahead. "That's a really pink house."

The Chateau rose above them in all of its pink glory, like some kind of 18th-Century Barbie Dreamhouse.

"It looks like it's sponsored by Pepto Bismol," said Randy.

"Dude, I could totally go for some Pepto Bismol right about now," Larry replied.

They walked around to the front of the building and climbed a short flight of stairs to the large wooden double door. In front of it they found a very large and very stony-faced individual in a black suit and sunglasses.

"Le château est fermé pour la fin du monde, messieurs."

"Uh...right," said Randy. "Do you, uhm, parlez the anglais?"

"Château is closed for end of world."

"Ah," said Larry. "Apparently everyone's already heard about all of the gigantic angry deities running around."

"Sir," said Randy. "The thing is, we're sort of...The One."

The man's expression didn't seem to change, but he raised his sunglasses and stared down at them thoughtfully.

"You are one?"

"We are two," said Randy. "But we are The One."

The guard tapped his earpiece. "Il y a des mecs qui disent qu'ils sont l'Un. Ouais. Ouais. No, ouais. Ehhh...chais pas. Comme des connards."

"He said something about ducks," Randy whispered to Larry.

"He said we look like a couple of assholes," Larry replied in his normal tone of voice.

"What? How do you even know that?"

"I play a lot of online multiplayer games at odd hours."

They waited while the guard finished his conversation. "Yes," the man said finally. "Welcome to Château de Voltaire. Follow me, if you please."

The entryway looked like a museum, with paintings and sculptures meeting the eye in every direction. The man detached a velvet rope from the brass stanchion blocking a grand marble staircase, and gestured for them to proceed up the stairs. He reattached the rope and followed behind them.

The upper level was equally ornate, and the guard led them to a chamber with two very tall beds covered with elaborate canopies.

"Dinner will be served in a few hours," said the guard. "I

149

am told that you may be tired from your travels. Please feel free to rest here for now. If you need something, you may simply shout. The house is not terribly large and I can hear...everything."

The bed was firm and surprisingly comfortable, and Randy was asleep in no time. With all that had happened in such a short period, he found himself transitioning liminally in and out of restless and troubling dreams.

Finally, after some indistinguishable period of time, he heard a strange rustling sound and felt a weight on top of his lower body.

"Mmbguhwahh," he mumbled dreamily. "Go away, Larry. I'm trying to—"

"AAAAAAAAH!" screeched what Randy quickly discovered to be a naked woman straddling his bed covers.

"AAAAAAAAH!" screeched Randy.

"You're not Voltaire!" the woman screamed.

"You speak English!" shouted Randy. "Also that's not important! Why would I be Voltaire?"

"Because I heard snoring in here, and I thought that—Hey, guy! Would you stop staring at my tits already?"

"I mean, it's just that they're right there..."

"Connard," the woman muttered, and with a strange flash of purplish light she vanished suddenly into thin air.

Randy stared at the space where the beautiful woman had been only moments before. "Well that can't be normal," he said.

"Larry!" he whispered.

"Go away, Randy," Larry muttered. "I'm trying to sleep."

Randy would have thought that that would be the end of such a peculiar matter, but as it turned out, strange women continued to materialize and dematerialize (each time accompanied by that odd flash of purple) for the better part of the next hour, while Larry continued to sleep through all of it. They appeared out of thin air sporting a wide variety of styles of dress and states of undress, and all reacted similarly to the first upon discovering that Randy was not the mysterious Voltaire for whom they were all apparently looking.

A confused tourist or two would be one thing, but with the sheer volume of traffic and the strange manner of entrance that brought the women, Randy thought that there must be something more to it. He began to suspect that a descendant of the famous philosopher who still bore his surname, or else perhaps a crafty conman, had taken up residence in the Chateau and was using it as the ultimate bachelor pad.

Randy tried to make conversation with some of the women, hoping to learn more about the bizarre situation, but it seemed that once they had discovered their mistake, they were inclined to engage their sparkly disappearing act post-haste without any further chit chat.

Finally, after what seemed like several hours of mysterious but decreasingly surprising apparitions, the familiar doorman appeared with a short, sharp double knock to which he didn't await a reply before entering.

"What time is it?" asked Larry, opening his eyes and sitting up.

"Wait, so *that's* what wakes you up?" Randy said incredulously. "This guy knocking? Not, say, all of the naked and seminaked women who have been parading through here for the last few hours?"

"Ah, the women," said the doorman.

"There were women?" asked Larry.

"There are always women, Monsieur," said the doorman. "Sometimes men also. And in response to your prior question, it is nearly dinnertime. I will be just outside the door, and when you are ready you may follow me to the dining room. In the meantime you will find two showers just through that door, and seeing as you are without bags, I have taken the liberty of putting some...fresher clothing for you in the wardrobe."

Randy and Larry looked down at themselves, and then at each other, each sniffing rather tentatively.

"Sorry, Sir," said Randy. "We were inside a whale."

"And not even that recently," added Larry.

"Indeed," said the doorman, stepping out quickly and with a look of some relief as he did so.

Behind the door they found a large and luxuriously equipped bathroom, with twin adjacent showers that had fogged glass on the lower half for an inkling of privacy.

"When in Rome," said Larry.

"You know we're not actually in Rome, though, right?" asked Randy.

"No idea where we are," said Larry, who was already naked and stepping into his shower. "So Randy, what was this you were saying about a bunch of naked wom—AAAAAAAAH! WHO ARE YOU AND WHY ARE YOU NAKED?"

"ME?" cried the woman. "WHO ARE YOU AND WHY ARE YOU NAKED?"

"Why is anyone naked, really, when you think about it?" Randy added.

Larry and the newcomer stopped. "WHAT?" they replied simultaneously.

"I mean, maybe don't think about it too much..." muttered Randy. "Hey, but like what's with all the weird flashing?"

The woman's face looked ready to explode. "I COULD ASK YOU THE SAME DAMN ohhh, you mean with the lights and the purple and all that?"

"Yes, that one," said Randy.

"You see," she explained, "that's a sort of natural reaction that occurs when—"

"Randy and Larry!" blurted Larry suddenly.

"What?" the woman asked, caught off guard.

"Er, because I said who are you, and you said who are we..." continued Larry. "So, yeah. We're Randy and Larry. He's Randy, and I'm Larry."

"Oh, I bet you are!" said the woman. "Welp. I've had about enough of this shit. Connards." And with a flash of electric purple, she was gone.

"Ohhhh," said Larry, "I see. The weird flashing. Huh. And then they just, like, disappear like that. Yeah, that can't be normal."

"Right?"

The doorman was waiting just outside their room, as promised. They followed him down the stairs and into a dining room that seemed extravagant yet tasteful. At one end of the moderately-sized dining table sat a single, and indeed a rather singular, figure.

He stood as they entered, allowing them to have a better look at his features. He must have been between thirty and thirty-five, and quite handsome. His playful eyes, rakish smile, somewhat elongated nose, and angular chin and jawline reminded Randy of paintings he had seen of the philosopher Voltaire, though this man was considerably younger, and he mentally placed a checkmark on the descendant theory. The man was wearing a gray linen shirt and gray linen pants, and his short, spiky hair was beginning to show signs of gray itself.

"Greetings," he said to them, with a thick French accent. "I am Voltaire. And you, as I understand, are now Z1."

"Z1?" they both inquired doubtfully.

"Ze One! Ze One! At least in zis particular world, yes?"

"Ah!" said Randy. "Ze One! Yes. That's us."

"At least that's what they tell us," said Larry. "And you, are you not from this particular world?"

"I am, and I am not," said Voltaire. "I am from zis world, and from all of ze possible worlds."

"Glad we cleared that up," said Larry. "Say, there were some naked girls looking for you."

"*Women*," reminded Randy.

"There were some naked women looking for you."

"Ah yes, ze womans," said Voltaire. "Zay hear it is end of world and zay want to make sexing with Voltaire for one last time, yes?"

"Sure, clearly," said Randy. "So...Voltaire. Are you, like, a descendant of the real Voltaire? I mean, you know. The philosopher?"

"I am Voltaire," said Voltaire. "Zere is just one, yes? François-Marie Arouet. Vous savez...Voltaire!"

"There's also the goth singer Voltaire," Larry suggested.

"Ah, yes," said Voltaire. "He is very good, yes? I am enjoying his song about killing ze man upstairs, is very witty. But still I am ze real Voltaire, en tous cas."

"You wrote, like, 'Candide,' and...stuff?" asked Randy. "It's just that all of that was a really long time ago, and you're..."

"Very sexy?" suggested Voltaire.

"I was going to say 'alive,' but sure," said Randy. "We can do your thing."

"Ah, yes, zis," said Voltaire. "I see zey did not explain all of zis to you. When you are a Traveler, ze Space and ze Time and all of zis are not so important. Zey are like small details, yes?"

"I'm not sure I follow," said Randy. "What sort of a traveler are you?"

"Like with ze spacetime zones, ze...how do you say, dimensions?"

"You're saying you're an interdimensional traveler?" asked Larry. "Like The Doctor or something?"

"Ze doctor who?"

"Exactly."

"What?"

"Alright," said Randy. "Rather than spend the next hour playing Doctor Who's on First, let's clarify what we know. So...Good ORB sent us here to hide out and get safe passage to Cosmic IDOL. The house is overrun by naked women trying to get a last round in with our friend Voltaire, who is apparently some kind of time-traveling interdimensional horndog."

"I like zis description very much! And now is time for dinner. If ze gods mean for some of ze worlds to be ending soon, we shall at least feast first on some of ze best cuisine zis region has to offer."

"Perfect, I'm starving!" said Larry. "Wait, is this going to be, like, snails and stuff?"

"No, I detest ze French food," said Voltaire. "We have ordered ze takeout from Dharma just down ze road, ze vindaloo is magnifique. Ah! Here it comes now."

The vindaloo was indeed magnifique, as were the lamb biryani, the korma, and the rest of it.

"So, you are British? I love ze British!" said Voltaire.

"Actually we're American," said Larry.

"Oh la la, ze American!" cried Voltaire. "I have a very good friend he is American, perhaps you are knowing him!"

"I mean, we don't all—" Randy started.

"He is called Benjamin Franklin!" Voltaire said excitedly. "He is always inventing ze things. You Americans, you are very clever! You know, Ben, he is ze one who introduce me to traveling ze dimensions."

"You don't say," muttered Randy, who was starting to lose his patience with their strange host and his stories.

"Yes, I was just a young man," continued Voltaire. "I was studying under ze Jesuits at Collège Louis-le-Grand when one day he just appear to me quite suddenly, out of nowhere, with ze most peculiar flash of purple electricity. And he say to me hello, old friend! Now, I do not recognize zis man, is long before all of ze French are knowing him as l'ambassadeur électrique. So he explain to me that he is friends with me far in ze future, when I am a dying old man. And he say that in ze future he has initiated me into his brotherhood of travelers of ze dimensions."

"Hey, interdimensional traveling Freemasons!" said Larry. "I saw that on the History Channel!"

"That is so not a thing," Randy grumbled.

"Oh!" said Larry. "Speaking of weird stuff, Mr. Voltaire, by any chance in your interdimensional travels have you ever seen one of these?" He pulled out the mysterious metallic sphere with shifting blue symbols that he had obtained at the shop in Tokyo.

"Ah!" said Voltaire. "I have indeed! But not for a very long time. Yes, quite a beautiful specimen zis is! You are quite fortunate to have found it."

"Awesome," said Larry. "So, like, what is it? What do I do with it?"

Voltaire nodded. "Zis you will know when ze time comes."

"Damn it!" Larry cried. "I'm so tired of knowing what to do with things when the time comes! Don't you people get it? I never know what to do with anything when the time comes!"

"Ah, I do not have zis problem," laughed Voltaire. "Zis is why ze womans are looking for Voltaire, yes?"

"Alright, fine," said Larry. "Go on with your story. What was Ben Franklin like?"

"In ze beginning I find him quite annoying, to be candid," said Voltaire. "He is so happy all of ze time, everything is always ze best. Voltaire, I just eat ze best food in all ze dimensions. Voltaire, I just sexing ze best woman in all ze dimensions. Voltaire, when you live in all of ze possible worlds at ze same time and taking ze best of each, you cannot help but live in ze best of all possible worlds. He is never shutting up."

"You didn't like him because he was happy?" Randy asked.

"Je suis Parisien!" Voltaire protested. "But zen he begins to teach me how to travel. He tells me ze dimensional travel, it requires much preparation. It is like ze meditation and ze yoga of l'Orient, yes? Preparing ze mind. For most it will take a lifetime dedicated only to zis. So when he is meeting me in ze future, it is too late, I have not ze time. So I tell him, and by zis I mean future me tells him, you see, I tell him I am done, let me rot in peace, go and find ze young Voltaire and teach him, he who has ze youth and ze time and ze energy, you see?"

"Absolutely!" Larry replied, while Randy just rolled his eyes.

"So it turns out I am learning ze travel very quickly, and soon I am traveling ze dimensions with ze Monsieur Franklin, discovering for myself ze best of all possible worlds. Experiencing all ze dimensions have to offer. And you know what? It is quite fucking good!" Voltaire laughed boisterously as though he'd just heard the greatest joke in all possible worlds.

"Ok," said Randy smugly, "so how does this interdimensional travel work, then?"

Voltaire laughed. "I see zat you do not believe me. You make fun of me."

"You got me," said Randy. "I don't believe you. I mean, look, this has got to be the most ridiculous story I've heard in at least a few hours."

"Tell me," laughed Voltaire, apparently not in the least offended, "what would you like to see as proof? Name it. Anything."

"Ooh! Who killed Tupac?" Larry asked.

Voltaire frowned. "I cannot tell you zis. Let us be reasonable."

"I want a baby dinosaur!" shouted Randy.

There was a short pause.

"Zis is weird, but ok," said Voltaire. There was a flash of electric purple, and he vanished.

And reappeared some seconds later, holding a stegosaurus roughly the size of a kitten. "Ok, it is kind of cute," he said, setting it down on the floor.

Randy and Larry stared at the dinosaur, mouths agape.

"So you just, like, went back in time and got a baby dinosaur?" Randy asked.

"No, no, don't be silly!" laughed Voltaire. "Traveling in time is very difficult and quite tiring. It is much easier to travel to one of ze many dimensions in which ze dinosaurs are still living, eh?"

"Oh, uh, sure. Obviously," said Randy, watching the creature waddle clumsily into the next room. "So, uh...go on?"

"Are you enjoying ze vindaloo?" asked Voltaire.

"Yes, it's fantastic!" said Randy.

"The best," agreed Larry.

"Zis is good," said Voltaire. "For when you are enjoying ze vindaloo, you are experiencing fully ze vindaloo. Ze vindaloo has a purpose, a character, a...vibration, you might say. A rhythm of life. Ze vindaloo is ze vindaloo, and when you are fully in ze vindaloo, you are...how do I say? You are sexing ze vindaloo."

"We're sexing the vindaloo?" Randy asked.

"I mean, it's good vindaloo, but..." Larry said.

"It is not just about ze vindaloo!" cried Voltaire. "Ze universe is made of many dimensions of experience, of purpose, of character. Dimensions of ze different frequencies, different vibration, you see?"

"Nope," said Larry.

"Not even a little bit," agreed Randy.

"When you are traveling ze dimensions," continued Voltaire, clearly quite enraptured with his own speech, "you are discovering ze rhythm, you are discovering ze vibration, you are joining with ze frequency of ze dimension in which you wish to insert yourself...you are sexing ze dimension."

"So, like, you and Ben Franklin are just running around sexing the universe?"

"Something like zis, yes," agreed Voltaire. "Of course as a young man my studies begin to suffer, but I do not say why to ze Jesuits. I think that ze Church will not like it so much."

"Écrasez l'Infâme!" Randy said, suddenly remembering Voltaire's famous motto regarding the Church. Crush the infamy.

"Ah, yes, zis," laughed Voltaire. "It is funny story, you know? One day I tell Ben I am meeting up with a woman and I am going to 'écraser la femme,' crush ze woman, you know? Like ze kids are saying 'smash' now, no? But Ben thinks I say 'Écrasez l'Infâme,' maybe his French is still a bit merdique, eh? Anyway, ze next thing I know everyone is telling me 'Écrasez l'Infâme' all ze time."

"Classic!" said Larry. "Hey, so with all of these infinite dimensions that you can travel to, how do you decide? Like, why are you here, now?"

"Ah, zis is a big question," Voltaire said. "I will tell you, having access to infinite dimensions can give you some serious FOMO, mofo! At least Ben likes to say it like zis, I am not certain I understand. But right now we are spending much of ze time here, because we have a project. Ben and I are working on upgrading and expanding our Large Hard-On Collider."

"Your what, now?" asked Larry.

"I think you mean the Large Hadron Collider," said Randy. "That is around here somewhere, isn't it?"

"It is right below our feet," said Voltaire, "and I mean just what I said. You see after many years, or perhaps many centuries of traveling, for one loses ze sense of time during such things, we had begun to discover ze techniques of science that could generate ze conditions conducive...ehhh...ze conducive conditions? Anyway, we discover how to make ze process easier. So in ze 1950s we create CERN, yes? And we begin to perfect ze technology, and eventually we create ze massive accelerator which makes a sort of interdimensional travel hot zone above ze twenty-seven kilometer circumference, so anybody in ze area can easily travel between dimensions with almost no training at all. Naturally we are building it in ze ground beneath chez moi, my house, because I always love to be hosting guests. So we are hoping it will become ze hotspot for interdimensional travel across ze universe, yes?"

"And did it?" asked Larry.

"Oh, yes did it!" Voltaire replied. "In fact, ze area around here was so full of travelers appearing out of nowhere, some on purpose and some by accident, that often zey would just crash into each other upon entry. And as I have explained about ze erotic energy involved in interdimensional travel, I should mention that for ze typical male human, ze crossing of ze dimensions often arouses a certain...je ne sais quoi, eh? So, Ben often is joking that we should be calling zis area ze Large Hard-On Collider."

"You've got to be shitting me," said Randy.

"I am not shitting," said Voltaire. "You see, later when we need to raise funding and make ze business seem legitimate to ze governments, we make up ze 'hadron' as just a group of particles zat already exist, and we just go back in time a little and seed zis idea into ze physics community and now we have ze Large Hadron Collider. But we are knowing ze real name."

"All this time travel...aren't you worried about creating a paradox?" asked Larry.

"A pair of ducks? Quels connards, I don't know anything about a pair of ducks. What ducks?"

"Nevermind," said Randy. "So tell us more about—"

KNOCK KNOCK KNOCK

Everyone looked in the direction of the front door. Silence ensued, followed by the muffled sound of a conversation.

"Maître Voltaire," said the doorman, as he entered the dining room. "Il y a un Monsieur Craig Kim dehors pour les deux connards."

"We understood that," Larry muttered.

"Let him in," said Voltaire.

There was a brief pause, and then there, in his full, douchey glory, was Craig Kim.

"Just what I fucking needed," said Randy.

"BAM! Rand-AY!" shouted Craig Kim, punching Randy on his upper arm. "How's it coming with that synergizing work?"

"I'm a little busy trying to save the world, Craig Kim!" said Randy. "What exactly are you doing here?"

"ORB sent me, to get you two to Cosmic IDOL," said Craig Kim. "Didn't they tell you? Thought everyone was on the same page. We're all hands on deck out here, working our action plans to keep this ship from sinking. Thinking outside of the box, my bro!"

"Is he always talking like zis?" asked Voltaire.

"Always," sighed Randy. "Voltaire, Craig Kim. Craig Kim, Voltaire."

"Enchanté," said Voltaire, shaking Craig Kim's hand firmly.

"Old champagne," agreed Craig Kim.

"They said they would send somebody for us in the morning," said Larry.

"Ah, right," said Craig Kim. "That was part of the game plan, just a bit of misdirection. Keep the enemy on their toes. But here I am, bro. Now it's showtime. Let's be laser focused and hit the ground running so we can get the most bang for our buck!"

"Is like I know ze words," said Voltaire, "but no meaning is behind zem. It is somehow familiar. Have we met before, Monsieur Craigkim?"

"Don't think we have, Brotaire," said Craig Kim.

"Are you a real human?" asked Voltaire.

"Yes, I am a real human," laughed Craig Kim. "I'm also an influencer, a thought leader, a game changer…"

"Ze words," said Voltaire. "So meaningless, yet so strangely hypnotic…"

"Well, I'm in Sales," said Craig Kim.

"Yes, naturally," said Voltaire, "and yet where have I heard such words?"

He paused again to think, and then, slowly but surely, a look of horror came into his eyes as his mouth fell agape.

"Nom de Dieu!" Voltaire whispered. "You. YOU! I have met you before! Many years ago. You are not Monsieur Craigkim. You are ze KRAKEN!"

"I knew it!" cried Randy.

"What?" Larry said. "No you didn't!"

"Well I knew he was a dick…"

161

"Quite an insight," said Larry. "Say, are you as lost as I am here?'

"Sooooo lost," said Randy.

"BWAAAAH HA HA HA HA HA HAAAAAA!" roared Craig Kim.

"Did he just 'Bwa ha ha?'" asked Randy. "Like, in real life?"

"I believe he did," agreed Larry.

"François-Marie Arouet," said Craig Kim. "I see you are still meddling in affairs that do not concern you."

"Are we in a Scooby Doo cartoon?" asked Larry.

"Yes!" shouted Craig Kim. "I am indeed what you pathetic mental miscreants have termed The Kraken, in its purest and most concentrated of a plethora of embodied forms!"

"Did he say he has a plethora?" asked Randy.

"You proved to be a minor inconvenience to me in another time and place, 'Voltaire,' but I did not bother to destroy you then. Do not think for a moment that I will prove so merciful again."

"Come on, now that bit just sounded like Star Wars," said Larry.

"My powers have increased since zis time," said Voltaire. "You will not find the battle as easy as you think."

"Maybe we should just go," said Larry.

"No!" said Craig Kim. "You two imbeciles are coming with me. And as for your new friend, this will only take a moment."

Craig Kim closed his eyes and appeared to concentrate deeply. At the same time, the look on Voltaire's face began to transform from one of mockery, to one of concern, and finally outright fear.

"No!" cried Voltaire. "You will not take control of my mind! Zees two are under my charge, and I will not allow you to take zem!"

"There will be little left of 'you' to allow or disallow anything in a matter of moments," laughed Craig Kim.

"You are indeed still too strong," said Voltaire, "and you have won zis time. But I assure you that there will come a

AHHHHHHHHHHH!"

"Save it for your Oscars speech," said Craig Kim. "For now, it's time to die."

"Never!" Voltaire cried, and with a blinding flash of electric purple he vanished without a trace.

"Not to worry," Craig Kim laughed. "I've sent a small, autonomous thread from my infinite mindstream to follow him and finish the job. Now, you two are coming with me, and if either of you has any opinions to share on the matter, then I will be happy to kill you both on the spot."

"Uh...cool," said Randy. "Carry on."

"We're good," agreed Larry.

PART 3: IDOL MINDS

30. KRAKEN THE CODE

"Well, it looks like you've got us, Craig Kim," said Larry. "So what are you planning to do with us?"

"I don't think ISIS would look kindly on you murdering The One right before Cosmic IDOL," said Randy.

By this point Craig Kim had marched them outside, and loaded them into his gigantic, bright yellow Hummer.

"Oh, they don't care," replied Craig Kim as he started the engine. "They don't concern themselves with the wellbeing of the contestants until they've arrived. And if nobody arrives, then your species forfeits."

"So that's it?" asked Randy. "This weird pink interdimensional hotspot is going to be the end of the road for Larry and me?"

"Not if I can help it!" cried Larry. "Don't move, asshole! I've got an EMF gun pointed at your head!"

"Unbelievable!" laughed Craig Kim.

"He means an EMP gun," Randy added helpfully.

And indeed, Larry had pulled out the EMP gun and was aiming it right at Craig Kim.

Craig Kim rolled his eyes. "Please. Do you think I've got as tenuous a hold on this host mind as your little octopus friends? Go ahead! Do it!"

"Oh, I'll do it!" shouted Larry.

"Then do it!"

"Oh, I will!"

"Dude, just do it already," said Randy.

So Larry pulled the trigger, and the EMP gun made the

same faint whirring noise as previously.

There was a pause.

"Now what?" asked Larry.

"Is he—?" Randy started.

"Still me, guys," said Craig Kim. "Now can we get on with this?"

"Uh...sure," said Larry. "Damn it. Go ahead and kill us, then."

"I'm not going to kill you," said Craig Kim. "For now."

"Then what?" asked Larry. "Kidnap us and hide us in a secure location until the competition has passed?"

"Not at all," said Craig Kim. "We're going to Cosmic IDOL!"

"Uh...why?" asked Larry.

"Isn't it obvious?" asked Craig Kim. "You see, if your ORB doesn't hear from you soon, they're bound to find some replacements. And the replacements are bound to be smarter than you two, because I mean..." He simply gestured in their direction.

"Gee, thanks," said Larry.

"What I don't get," said Craig Kim, "is why is it still you two, anyway? You were meant to be decoys, right? Red herrings to keep us off the trail of the real One. Hawking and the Lama."

"They would've been so much better than us," said Larry.

"Right?" Craig Kim agreed. "But we saw through the trick, and we captured them. Now your ORB is saying you're all they have left, and they seem to be going out of their way to get you to Cosmic IDOL. But why? Why not just grab the nearest two humans at the last minute?"

Randy and Larry paused to think about that.

"Well?" asked Randy. "You're the ancient, immortal genius. You tell us why."

Craig Kim frowned. "I don't know. It just doesn't make sense. Maybe they don't want to subject some random humans to this bizarre scenario on such short notice. But then why not use some of their own ORB people who already know what's happening? Or maybe you two are actually some kind of geniuses and this whole moron thing is just another mildly clever ruse."

"Oh, I can assure you that's not it," said Larry.

"Well whatever it is, I intend to find out. And then I'll most likely just kill you both. So, shall we get going?"

"Well, if you put it like that..." said Randy.

"Hey, Craig Kim," said Larry, "what happened to your bro-speak?"

"Oh, that was just a tool," said Craig Kim. "It has a sort of hypnotic effect on the human brain that puts you into a state of reduced prefrontal cortex activity, overriding your logical reasoning and making you more open to suggestion. It's great for working in Sales, but also extremely annoying to keep up for any period of time, for one who is, in fact, neither a human nor a bro."

"So were we even in school together?" asked Randy.

"Hell if I know," said Craig Kim. "It's unlikely. I just found this guy while probing random minds on the street, and I liked his name."

"Son of a bitch," said Randy.

"So where exactly does Cosmic IDOL take place, anyway?" Larry asked. "They only said we'd be walking across the border into Switzerland to avoid detection."

"Oh, we won't be walking," said Craig Kim. "I want everyone to know I'm coming and that I've got you two with me. Anyway, Cosmic IDOL is taking place at the only venue on Earth suited to hosting an event of this magnitude."

"Which is?"

"Atlantis, of course."

"Oh, sure, of course, Atlantis!" said Randy. "The ancient, sunken island nation that Plato made up for an allegory. Why didn't I think of that?"

"Didn't Doris say something about the Atlanteans?" said Larry. "Something about them being Neanderthals?"

"Ah, yes," replied Craig Kim. "The Atlanteans are Neanderthals."

"Right, that was the one," said Larry.

"They're that bad?" asked Randy.

"Bad?" asked Craig Kim. "They're fantastic! The level of client service and event management that they provide is absolutely unequaled. How amazing would it be if they were still ruling the Earth's land masses, instead of you people?"

"Randy, are you as lost as I am?" asked Larry.

"Twice as," said Randy. "Here, let me try. Craig Kim... Whuh?"

"Ok," said Craig Kim. "I can see that your ORB had you two on a need-to-know basis with these things, so let me explain. You're familiar with Neanderthals?"

"I mean, not personally," said Randy.

"I know a few," said Larry.

"So you're aware," said Craig Kim, "that the Neanderthals disappeared roughly 40,000 years ago, after some period of interaction with homo sapiens?"

"Sure," said Randy.

"I'm going to say yes, just to keep things moving," said Larry.

"Well," said Craig Kim, "what happened is, around that time, some ISIS representatives decided that Earth would be a perfect location for a really massive intergalactic event venue. Specifically, the inside part of the Earth."

"OMG, you're one of those Hollow Earther nuts!" laughed Larry.

"However," continued Craig Kim, ignoring the interruption, "ISIS's non-colonialism policy required them to obtain an uncoerced agreement from the most intelligent species residing on the planet."

"Ok, so did we agree?" asked Randy.

"Actually, the most intelligent species they found were the Neanderthals."

"Hey!" cried Larry.

"The leader of the Neanderthals at the time was King Atlas. He told the ISIS representatives that he and his people were looking for somewhere better to live, as they were not happy with the direction the neighborhood was going in, what with all the humans moving in."

"Hey!" cried Randy and Larry together.

"So, King Atlas agreed to let the ISIS representatives have their intergalactic convention center inside the planet, on the condition that the Neanderthals would move to the center of the Earth and run the venue themselves. And that's the real reason you see the Neanderthals disappear so quickly from the archaeological record. Plato describes this event in coded language, with Atlantis sinking beneath the sea. And the concentric circles he talks about in his description of Atlantis are, of course, the Earth's layers leading down to the core."

Larry laughed. "That's got to be the dumbest story I've heard in at least the last twenty minutes or so."

"Ok, so Cosmic IDOL is at an event venue inside the Earth, run by Neanderthals," said Randy. "But then why do we have to go into Switzerland to get in?"

"Well," said Craig Kim. "Have you ever heard of the Swiss bunkers?"

"Ooh!" shouted Larry. "I saw a show on that! They have, like, thousands of hidden underground bunkers all over the country, in case of war or nuclear attacks."

"Exactly," said Craig Kim. "Only, that's not what they're actually for. In reality, those bunkers are the entrances to Atlantis."

"Hold on, that doesn't make sense," said Randy. "If there are thousands of bunkers across the country with however many people maintaining them...everyone in Switzerland would have to be in on it!"

"Not everyone," said Craig Kim. "Just the Swiss."

"So all of the Swiss are in on this massive Hollow Earth conspiracy?" asked Larry.

"What you have to understand about the Swiss, is..." Craig Kim seemed to hesitate. "How shall I put this?"

"Just put it," said Larry.

"They're a sophisticated and ruthless race of beings originating from the Helvetios star system roughly fifty light-years from Earth, frequently employed by ISIS for their protection services."

"That is the dumbest thing I've heard in approximately three minutes," said Randy.

"So...Swiss people are some kind of intergalactic bouncers?" asked Larry.

"Bouncers, guards, wealth management advisors..." said Craig Kim. "In this case they manage admission to one of the most heavily trafficked event venues in the known universe while keeping the whole thing entirely secret from the general population of the planet."

"Ok," said Randy, "I guess that sounds kind of difficult."

"Ah, here we are coming to the Swiss border now," said Craig Kim.

They slowed down as they approached a nondescript building, where a guard looked up at the massive yellow monstrosity that they were riding in and immediately signaled for them to stop.

"Hi!" said Craig Kim to the guard before he could even open his mouth. "Are you the French guy or the Swiss guy?"

"I am ze French guy."

"You will get me the Swiss guy," said Craig Kim.

"I will get you ze Swiss guy," said the French guy, and walked away.

"Whoa," said Larry. "Did you just Jedi mind trick that guy?"

"Something like that."

Another guard arrived. "Yes?" he asked.

"You will get a message to ISIS and the humans," said Craig

Kim.

"Do I look like Facebook to you?" sneered the guard. "Tell them yourself."

Craig Kim reached into the glove box and brought out a heaping double handful of what appeared to be diamonds. "I need you to get a message to ISIS and the humans. Please."

"These are real?" asked the guard. "None of that synthetic bullshit?"

"Structurally they're the same thing!" said Craig Kim. "They taste exactly the same!"

"You eat a lot of diamonds?" asked the guard.

"Well, no, obviously not."

"Right, obviously not," said the guard. "So how about I don't lecture you on the culinary differences between shrimp and prawns, and you don't try to tell me which precious stones taste the same."

"How'd you know I was a cephalopod?"

"You don't get to be the galaxy's premier protection-for-hire service without being observant," said the guard. "Now, what brand is that purse?"

"It's not a purse," said Craig Kim, "it's a men's weekender bag."

"Well, isn't that precious. Brand and material?"

"Givenchy. Grained leather."

The guard smiled. "Sounds delicious," he said.

"Fine," said Craig Kim, and began dumping his papers and belongings out of the bag. "Now, I want you to tell them that Craig Kim is an incarnation of the Kraken, and that he's got Randy and Larry hostage. And if anyone tries to stop me, I'm killing them both."

"Awesome," said Randy.

"And otherwise, if nobody tries anything, you intend to do what with them?" asked the guard.

"None of your business," said Craig Kim. "Oh, and listen. I want them to know about this, but I don't want them to know that I know that they know."

"Done," said the guard, snatching the designer man bag from Craig Kim's reluctant grasp. "I'll get the word out right now. Nice doing business with you."

Craig Kim restarted the engine and drove across the border.

"So," said Larry. "That dude's just gonna, like, eat your man sack?"

"Unfortunately," said Craig Kim. "If you've ever been in a Swiss city or airport, you'll notice that there are shops everywhere selling jewelry, designer handbags, and watches, but it's really hard to find food. The Helvetians can process human food when it's necessary, but they much prefer their native diet of precious stones and designer fabrics."

"Ok," said Randy. "Weird. So, why did you just give away the fact that you've captured us?"

Craig Kim smiled. "Because I want to see everyone's reaction," he said.

31. JOURNEY TO THE CENTER OF THE EARTH

Craig Kim drove them further into Switzerland in the gaudy yellow Hummer. Soon he turned away from the main road and began driving down small country roads, surrounded by green pastures and farmland. They could see mountains in the distance on all sides. Eventually, they pulled to the side of the road in what seemed to be the precise geographical center of nowhere.

They exited the car and found themselves at the bottom of a densely wooded hill.

"Just up there, at that rock outcropping," said Craig Kim. "we'll find a bunker."

They hiked their way up the steep incline, making their own path as they went, and after about fifteen minutes they came to the start of the rocky area. Sure enough, a tall, steel double door stood before them.

Craig Kim found a panel with what appeared to be an old intercom system, and pushed the button.

"Mot de passe?" came a voice immediately.

"Team Cephalo," said Craig Kim.

"Entrez," said the voice, and the steel doors slid apart to the sides like the entrance to a mall.

The inside, however, was anything but a mall. Before

them stretched a long, concrete and steel tunnel with minimal lighting. Somewhere water was dripping loudly onto metal. One of the light panels on the ceiling flickered on and off continuously, giving the air of a low-budget slasher flick. The overall effect was less than inviting.

"You sure this is the right place?" Larry asked.

"Don't worry," said Craig Kim. "It's nicer downstairs. There are too many of these entrances to properly maintain them all, plus they need to keep up appearances."

They walked down the long tunnel for what seemed like several miles, their steps echoing loudly as they went. Finally, Craig Kim stopped.

"This should be it," he said, indicating a dimly lit side corridor that Randy and Larry had barely noticed as they walked past it.

They turned that way, and soon found themselves in an empty room with bare concrete walls, and no entrances or exits other than the one they had come from. It didn't look very promising.

"*REGISTERED EVENT GUESTS DETECTED,*" came a soothing feminine voice. "*WELCOME, RANDY. WELCOME, LARRY. WELCOME, CRAIG KIM. WELCOME, PRE-AUTHORIZED SECONDARY MINDSTREAM.*"

"Uh...thanks?" said Larry.

The room lit up with soft blue and green lights that seemed to come from everywhere and nowhere at once.

"Just for the record, Craig Kim is holding us hostage," said Randy.

"*PLEASE ADDRESS ANY CONCERNS TO A GUEST SERVICES ASSOCIATE, WHO CAN BE RECOGNIZED BY THEIR DISTINCTIVE BLUE AND GREEN UNIFORMS AND THEIR ELECTRONIC BADGE WITH THE WORDS 'GUEST SERVICES ASSOCIATE' DISPLAYED IN YOUR LANGUAGE OF PREFERENCE.*"

"Cool, thank you," said Randy. "I'll be sure to do that."

"*COMMENCING DESCENT TO ATLANTIS.*"

A concrete door slid shut across the entrance they had

come from, but then nothing seemed to happen.

"Isn't it like four thousand miles to the Earth's core?" asked Randy.

"Roughly," said Craig Kim.

"So won't that take a week or two in an elevat—"

"*NOW ARRIVING AT ATLANTIS.*"

"Apparently no," said Craig Kim.

The door slid back open, and Randy and Larry followed Craig Kim out into a world unlike anything they had ever witnessed.

The first impression of Atlantis was one of being surrounded on all sides by life and lights and joyful sounds.

Everywhere one looked there were living creatures walking, crawling, swimming, or flying. Many appeared human or humanoid, but of these there was such diversity of coloring, facial features, limbs, wings, and other protrusions that it seemed almost impossible for them all to have emerged from the same process of evolution. Besides these there were other beings that vaguely resembled the insects, reptiles, birds, and sea life with which Randy and Larry were familiar, others that appeared more like trees or plants or minerals, many that seemed to be mechanical or biomechanical. Some were simply outside of the realm of anything that they had words or concepts for.

And the lights! As Craig Kim had explained, Atlantis existed at the core of the Earth, and so as they looked around, they quickly realized that they were walking upon the inner surface of a sphere. The sphere must have been only a few dozen miles in diameter because they could clearly see its curvature in the distance all around them. The ground was covered in streets and buildings like in a regular city, but the architecture was quite alien to them. The buildings were made up mostly of clear or translucent domes of various sizes, and these emitted soft blue and green lights, much like the ones they had seen in the elevator. These lights extended among the buildings on the streets surrounding them, and then up with the curvature of the sphere, and filled the walls of the sphere around and above them, so that the entire sky above was a vast field of domes and lights.

And scattered about within that soft blue and green glow that seemed to be an inherent part of the building materials in Atlantis, there were colorful electronic signs, much like those in Times Square or Tokyo or a thousand other places on Earth. These were advertising hotels, restaurants, bars, casinos, and souvenir shops.

In addition to the buildings and lights that extended all the way up the surface of the sphere on all sides and above their heads, there were bubbles floating around in the air, and inside of them were more shops, restaurants, floating parties, and electronic billboards.

"It's funny that the signs are all in English," said Randy.

"Everyone sees them in their own preferred language," replied Craig Kim.

"Right, that reminds me, I need to find one of those Guest Services Associates."

"They won't help you."

"So the gravity continues all the way up there?" Larry said, pointing overhead. "Like, we could just walk up to there from here?"

"Yes," said Craig Kim. "ISIS has used technologies far beyond your comprehension to manipulate the gravitational fields such that there is a pull toward the inner surface of the sphere on all sides. In addition, each visitor feels the exact level of gravitational force that they are most accustomed to, to maximize the comfort of Atlantis's guests. However the field only extends close to the surface, so if you kick off forcefully, you'll float up into the zero-G center of the city, where all of those bubbles are floating around."

"Sounds pretty nifty," said Larry.

He noticed then that just around the center of the Atlantis sphere, floating through empty space with all of the bubbles, was a massive platform holding what must have been several thousand people and aliens, surrounding a raised stage. A video screen backdrop showed a magnified image of the stage for those in the surrounding sphere, and enormous speakers projected the glorious, funky sounds in every direction.

"Is that...Jamiroquai?" asked Larry.

"I think so," said Randy. "And that other guy playing with him...who is that, one of those rainbow-colored mumble rappers or something?"

"That's George Clinton, you dumbass!" said Larry.

"I mean, who did you guys think would be headlining Cosmic IDOL?" asked Craig Kim.

"I kind of thought...nobody?" said Randy.

"I don't know what I thought," said Larry. "But this music!"

"This may be the greatest sound that's ever been in my ears," Randy agreed.

"I told you guys," said Craig Kim, "these Neanderthals know their event planning."

"Oh, hey!" said Randy. "There's one of those customer service people now. Excuse me! Excuse me, Sir!"

The green and blue uniformed individual he was addressing looked human at first glance, but then Randy noticed his strong, stocky build and slightly odd facial features, including a pronounced cranium.

"Dude," Larry said, in what may have been an attempt at a whisper. "He's one of those Neanderthals!"

"Yes," said the Neanderthal, clearly not amused. Then, turning to Craig Kim and indicating Randy and Larry with a dismissive gesture, he said "Are these yours, Sir?"

"They're with me at the moment," said Craig Kim.

"He's kidnapped us," added Randy. "That's what I wanted to talk to you about."

"Why is it speaking at me?" asked the Guest Services Associate. "Homo sapiens are generally not allowed at this venue, you know."

"I'm aware," said Craig Kim, "but given the particulars of this event I'm guessing you've been forced to make some exceptions?"

"Yes, unfortunately," said the Associate.

"Well," said Craig Kim, "these ones happen to be contestants. They're The One."

The Associate looked them up and down, then suddenly broke out in laughter. "These two? Well, good luck with that, then!" And he walked away.

"Well, that was helpful," said Larry.

"I thought you said their level of client service was unequaled," said Randy.

"Sure," said Craig Kim. "Just...not for you people, specifically."

"Alright, then," said Randy. "Apparently nobody's planning to rescue us. So, what now?"

"Now," said Craig Kim, "we get to find out just what in the hell is going on around here. And to do that, we'll need to meet up with some friends of mine."

"You have friends?" asked Larry.

"Well, technically they're all me."

"Ah," said Randy. "That makes a lot more sense. So where do a bunch of copies of you meet up with each other?"

"At the darkest, sketchiest back-alley bar known to the center of the Earth," said Craig Kim, and then he paused for dramatic effect. "Boys, we're going to the Con Cave."

"The concave?" asked Randy. "I don't get it. This entire place is concave. Also, did you just pause for dramatic effect?"

"No!" growled Craig Kim. "Nobody does that! And it's 'Con Cave,' two words."

"Oh, like a cave at a convention center?" asked Larry.

"Ah, right," said Randy.

"NO NOT LIKE A CAVE AT A CONVENTION CENTER!" shouted Craig Kim. "It's a sketchy bar. Catering to shady individuals. Many of whom are career criminals. And it's located on the inner surface of a sphere. So it's the Con Cave. Ok?"

"Ok, geez," Larry sighed. "I hope the rest of the cons there are less sensitive than you are."

32. CON VEXED

The Con Cave turned out to be considerably brighter and shinier than the name implied. While the exterior dome was somewhat more opaque than most of the ones surrounding it, the interior was made entirely of the translucent substance with an internal blue and green glow that gave most of Atlantis its distinctive appearance. Up close they could see that the lights seemed to wander around lazily like living things, though it was difficult to pinpoint their actual source. The bar itself and the round bench tables were simply outcroppings of the same material, that seemed to grow out of the ground in an almost organic fashion.

"I don't see my friends yet," said Craig Kim, looking around.

"You know, you can keep using that word," said Larry, "but that doesn't make it any more true..."

They picked an open table and sat down to wait.

And wait they did.

And wait.

"So, you said this was a table service place?" asked Randy.

"Yes," replied Craig Kim. "I've been here many times. It definitely is."

Larry grabbed a drink menu from one of the nearby tables, and they all looked through it.

"I guess we probably shouldn't drink if we're doing this contest thing soon," said Larry.

"Actually," said Randy, "studies show that critical thinking and problem solving skills increase with alcohol intake, up to a certain point. And then decrease really quickly from there."

"So how do we know how much to drink?" asked Larry.

"Well, I guess we would just have to solve for—"

"Guys," Craig Kim interrupted. "You do realize that once I figure out what your ORB friends are really up to here, I'll probably just kill you before IDOL even starts."

"Drinking it is!" said Larry.

"Now, how do we choose, here?" asked Randy. "They say what all's in each drink but I've literally never heard of a single one of these ingredients."

"Of course," said Craig Kim. "None of them exists on Earth. Well, except here at Atlantis, where they have them shipped in. Anyway, just pick a name you like and order, everything is pretty good here."

"Hey, look," said Larry. "That hot waitress over there is checking me out."

"The Neanderthal?" asked Craig Kim.

"What? She's not a Neanderthal," said Larry. "Look how hot she is!"

"I guess she's attractive as far as you primates go. But yes, she's a Neanderthal. Many of them are pretty indistinguishable from you all. In any case, she's not checking you out, she's glaring at us. Because you two are homo sapiens, and she probably can't tell that I'm not one." He signaled to her, and she came over.

"What?" she asked.

"Hi," said Craig Kim with a smile. "We'd like to order some drinks, please."

"Go ahead," the waitress growled. "This whole place has obviously gone to shit anyway."

"Charming," said Craig Kim. "I'll have the Con Tempt."

"I'll go for the Con Fusion," said Randy.

"And I'll have the Con Test," said Larry.

The waitress walked away without a word.

"She's going to spit in our drinks, isn't she?" Randy asked.

"If we're lucky," said Craig Kim.

◆ ◆ ◆

"This drink is delicious!" said Randy. "It's really too bad I'll never be able to get one again."

"Neither can most of the interstellar visitors," said Craig Kim. "All of the drinks on the menu here are illegal on their planet of origin. It's kind of a theme."

"Illegal?" asked Larry. "Why are they irreeble? Ireever. Wafooba?"

"You guys, I feel weird," said Randy. "Do you guys feel weird?"

"Bawaba," agreed Larry.

"Oh look, my friends are here," said Craig Kim.

A group of about a dozen small children with shaved heads and identical white linen shirts and pants walked in and marched toward them in a single-file line.

"Larry!" Randy whisper-yelled. "How many of those things are you seeing?"

"Pafow," said Larry.

"Gentlemen, meet the Krak Babies," said Craig Kim.

"The what, now?" asked Randy.

"I know," said Craig Kim. "It wasn't our first choice. We wanted to call them the Kraken Kids, but apparently that's some Minecraft thing or something. And then we thought about Kraklings but that was half a dozen other things. Hey, remember before Google, when you could just not know that everything was already a thing?"

"Yeah, I do miss that," said Randy. "Question. Is this room expanding and contracting like really rapidly? Because it's kinda freaking me out!"

"Nope," said Craig Kim. "We grow them in a lab, you see. Krak Babies, this is Randy and Larry."

"Nice to meet you," said Randy. "Do you kids feel weird?"

"No," the Krak Babies all said in unison.

"Are you sure?" asked Randy with a puzzled expression.

"Because you look pretty weird to me. But you know what, though?"

◆ ◆ ◆

"You ok there, bud?" asked Larry.

"Oh hey, you can talk properly again," said Randy. "Yeah, I'm fine. I think. I don't know. Why?"

"Just because you said 'But you know what, though?' and then you went catatonic for like an hour and a half."

"What?"

"We've just kind of been sitting here the whole time," said Craig Kim. "And it got even more awkward with the waitress than it already was."

"Huh," said Randy. "Well, I guess we solved one problem, at least. The optimal number of illegal alien cocktails to have before a competition is none."

"Alright," said Craig Kim. "Well I guess now we can get on with it."

"With what?" asked Randy.

"Yeah, you didn't really tell us why we're here," said Larry.

"You're here for Cosmic IDOL," said Craig Kim.

"Right," said Randy, "but why are we in this bar with the Children of the Corn?"

"Because I have to get into your girlfriend's head."

"First of all, she's not my girlfriend, and second of all, whuh?"

"Look," said Craig Kim. "My kidnapping you will have set off all the alarm bells at ISIS and ORB, and right now Kali will be meeting with others to discuss their plans. Everyone thinks that private meetings are fully secure in Atlantis, but I don't have to tap into their conference room. I can just tap directly into their mindstreams. Compromising the mental integrity of a GOD is hard work, of course, which is why I called in my backup team. Now, our target is Kali because she'll be the easiest."

"What? Why?" asked Randy. "Because she's a woman?"

"Do you ever shut up with that stuff?" asked Craig Kim. "It's because I've known her well for many years through my work at ORB, which makes it easier to establish the connection."

"Oh. Right." said Randy. "Hey, you guys, I'm feeling less weird."

"This conversation is making you feel less weird?" asked Larry.

"Yeah, no, this conversation is super weird, obviously," said Randy. "But I think the intergalactic booze has mostly worn off. Hey, speaking of weird, if you've known Kelli well for so many years, why didn't she notice that you're an ancient cephalopod intelligence inside a human body? Everyone else seems to notice. Voltaire, that Swiss border guard..."

"That Guest Services Associate," Larry added.

"No, see, it's...you see...because..." Craig Kim paused for a minute with a pensive look. "Holy shit, that is kind of weird."

"Well?" said Larry. "What do you think it means?"

"Only one way to find out," said Craig Kim. "We're going in."

33. THE GODS EXPOSED

It was a small room with heavy concrete walls.

"I'm telling you, this is bullshit you guys," Kelli was saying. They couldn't see her, because they were looking through her eyes and listening with her ears. "ISIS isn't giving the humans a fair chance. They don't know them like I do! There's something special about this species. Anyway, I've had enough. I already told them, I'm resigning as soon as this thing is over."

"What?" asked a handsome old man with white hair, a white beard, and a white robe. They recognized him as Yahweh, only shrunken down to normal human size. "They like you, Kali. You have a bright future in ISIS, not like us. You think they'll give me or this overgrown sea slug another gig after all the regulations we've violated on this planet? We're done! We'll be lucky if they don't put us right back in the slammer."

"Speak for yourself, old man!" laughed Cthulhu, who was just as hideous and just as eldritch as the last time they'd seen him, but also now man-sized. "Anyway, you're wasting your breath. Kali hasn't been thinking straight ever since she developed a crush on that weird little human."

"Oh, piss off!" said Kelli. "I'm the only one of us who's thinking straight right now. Does any of this seem fair to you? Can't you see we've been played just as much as we've been playing these humans and cephalopods?"

"And?" asked Yahweh. "So what? It's one botched job. You

know we work on a need-to-know basis, just like everyone else in the organization. But you've forgotten that, because you let your emotions get the best of you. You've gotten too attached to your host species, and forgotten who you really work for! In any case, you've still done things by the book all along, and they notice that sort of thing. You can have any post you want after this! Just take a long vacation, and then I promise you, you can definitely find something a lot nicer than this shithole."

"I chose this shithole!"

"Fine, just throw it all away," Yahweh sighed. "Alright, so now what? We've been talking in circles for like an hour and a half. What do we need to do about this situation?"

"Nothing at all!" said Cthulhu. "We only need to keep them occupied for another hour or so and it'll be done. Right, Kali?"

"We can talk freely," said Craig Kim. "They can't hear us in here, and I've activated the shield of silence around our table at the Con Cave."

"Good to know," said Randy.

"Why is it just these three?" Craig Kim wondered aloud. "These are the General Operational Directors for the humans and the cephalopods, but where are all the higher-ups from ISIS? They should be in this meeting too!"

"I said right, Kali?" repeated Cthulhu.

"What?" asked Kelli, shaking her head, and with it their perspective. "Sorry, I was distracted for a moment."

"I said as long as they stay occupied for the next hour or so, we're good," said Cthulhu.

Kelli paused as though in thought.

"And by 'they,'" she said, "you mean the human contestants, as well as the cephalopod contestants, and their handlers at the respective ORBs."

"Yes," said Cthulhu. "I thought that was pretty clear."

"Because as we all know, Randy and Larry, who are The One for the humans, and The Kraken and whoever is replacing Paul, who are representing the cephalopods, have all come here to Atlantis for the purpose of participating in Cosmic IDOL."

"Uhm...correct," said Yahweh. "Are you feeling ok, Kali?"

"What is she doing?" asked Craig Kim.

"And as you're well aware," Kelli continued, "all of us now know that Craig Kim, who has been working as an operative at Human ORB, is in fact an avatar of The Kraken. And now he has kidnapped Randy and Larry, and brought them with him here to Atlantis."

"Yes, Kali," said Cthulhu. "We literally know everything that you're telling us right now."

"FORCED EXPOSITION!" Larry shouted. "She's forced exposing herself!"

"What?" asked Craig Kim.

"But why..." Randy started.

"Because she knows we're here!" Larry laughed.

"That's it!" said Randy. "And she wants us to know that she knows we're here..."

"Huh," said Craig Kim. "Oops."

"Look," said Kelli. "I'm just establishing the known facts, so that everyone present here can be on the same page, and come up with a smart path forward."

"Uh...ok," said Yahweh. "Seems a bit awkward and unnatural, but suit yourself."

"I always do," said Kelli. "So, as we all know, the humans and the cephalopods of Earth are not now, nor have they ever been, considered as serious candidate species for membership in ISIS."

"Right," said Cthulhu.

"Obviously," said Yahweh.

"WHAT?!" cried Randy, Larry, and Craig Kim.

"And of course," continued Kelli, "this Cosmic IDOL being held here at Atlantis is just an elaborate ploy to keep them distracted."

"Uh huh," said Yahweh.

"Yep," agreed Cthulhu.

"Son of a—!" yelled Craig Kim.

"Hey, can I just stop you there?" asked Yahweh. "I really need to pee."

"Let's take five and regroup," said Cthulhu. "Maybe Kelli will figure out where she's going with this."

Kelli got up to stretch, and they found their perspective staring idly at the walls as Yahweh left the room, and Cthulhu paced around nervously.

"Can she hear us?" asked Randy.

"I don't think so," said Craig Kim. "I think she just senses our presence somehow. Apparently even with the help of the Krak Babies, my powers are not quite what I thought them to be."

"Nice work there, Craig Kim!" laughed Larry. "So, what are they talking about with this ploy stuff?"

"It's almost like...wait!" cried Randy. "Do you remember that crazy old man in London? What did he say to us?"

"I don't know," said Larry. "Just a lot of gibberish about our friends becoming enemies and enemies becoming friends. Oh, and beware of..." his eyes widened.

"Beware of false idols!" said Randy.

"I don't know what you two are on about," said Craig Kim, "but that's some pretty impressive foreshadowing right there."

"Right?" said Larry. "Speaking of which, wouldn't it be funny if next week's class was on foreshadowing?"

"Poor or excessive use of foreshadowing is certainly a hallmark of bad writing," agreed Randy. "I bet it will be! In any case, I guess we'll know what the theme of next week's class is when the time comes."

"I'm back, you guys," said Yahweh. "Sorry about that."

"No problem," said Kelli. "So, as I was saying, we're all aware that this Cosmic IDOL is a fake, and that in fact ISIS is planning to accept the coral reefs as a new member species, as has been the plan now for millions of years, at the true Cosmic

IDOL ceremony taking place just off the coast of Sydney, Australia roughly one hour from now."

"Sure," said Yahweh.

"Uh huh," said Cthulhu.

"Goddamnit," Craig Kim sighed.

"Coral reefs?" asked Larry. "What, like, the whole reef? Wait, is this like an 'Avatar' forest kind of thing?"

Randy looked at him incredulously. "Are you talking about neural networks and distributed intelligence?"

"I don't know, is your thing that you just said like my thing that I just said?"

"Yes," said Randy.

"Then yes," agreed Larry.

"So, listen," Kelli said. "If the human One and the cephalopod representatives were to leave here and somehow make their way to the real Cosmic IDOL within the next hour, then we might have a problem."

"I feel like maybe we should leave here and somehow make our way to the real Cosmic IDOL within the next hour," said Craig Kim.

"Wow," said Randy. "What a brilliant idea you've just had there all by yourself, Craig Kim."

"Those who are your enemies will become your allies..." mumbled Larry.

"Damn it!" said Randy. "Now I have to work with Craig Kim? Ok, what else did that crazy old man say? Maybe there's a clue about what the hell we're supposed to actually do here."

"I think something about in the final hour we have to make our greatest weakness into a strength."

"Well, it sounds like this is the final hour," said Craig Kim. "So what's you guys's greatest weakness?"

"Wow, that's a tough one," said Randy. "We just have so many..."

"So, so many..." Larry agreed. "Anyway, how the hell should we know? We were just the red herrings to throw you off from the real contestants, for a fake contest! We're obviously too stupid for any of this!"

"Too stupid?" said Craig Kim. "Hmmm..."

"What problem?" asked Cthulhu. "What do you think these idiots could even do if they showed up in Sydney?"

"Beats me," said Kelli, "but there must be something, if the higher-ups were willing to release you two, and had us spend all this time and energy on distracting them with this fake competition. You know, if they were really clever, they might try something like—"

"Wait!" Cthulhu interrupted. "Hold on. Do you guys feel that?"

"Feel what?" asked Yahweh.

Cthulhu paused, appearing to concentrate intently. "There's something...there's...there's another mind in here! I can feel it. It's a...a cephalopod mind."

"Ooh, look at the time!" Craig Kim said. "Gotta run!"

"Well, shit, you guys," said Craig Kim, back at the Con Cave. "I guess they know we heard all that. So they know we'll be trying to get out of Atlantis and reach Sydney. Which means that even if we use the fastest UFOs or hypersonics that either ORB has, they're going to catch us before we ever get there."

"What do you think Kelli was about to suggest we do?" said Randy.

"Who knows?" Larry replied. "Hey, that was funny how she used forced exposition like that!"

"Yeah, so what was all that about?" Craig Kim asked.

"It's from our writing class," said Randy. "See, our teacher Judy has these Eight Elements of Bad Writing. It's sort of a what not to do kind of thing. The first class was on Cliches and Tropes. Like, say you had to somehow interrupt an alien plot to destroy mankind. You shouldn't do something that has been done a million times before, like, I don't know..."

"Hackers!" said Larry. "Infiltrating their alien hive mind

or whatever."

"Right," said Randy. "And then there was Literary Chauvinism, so basically it would be all dudes solving the problem. Next was Unnatural Dialog, which is the one that had forced exposition, and then we missed the class on Mixed Metaphors, but I guess you'd mix some different ideas together into a sort of incomprehensible mess. We also missed the Lazy Plotting session, but apparently they did an exercise on deus ex machina. So you'd pull some kind of last-minute solution out of your ass that didn't seem remotely plausible. And we don't know yet what the last three are."

"Ah," said Craig Kim. "Well that was...informative. But what does bad writing have to do with our real-world problem?"

"I have no idea," said Randy. "But I think I have an idea."

"That doesn't even make sense," said Craig Kim. "You have no idea, but you have an idea?"

"I have no idea what the answer to your question is," said Randy. "But I think I have an idea for how to solve our dilemma. I thought that was pretty clear."

"That was not at all clear."

"I got it," said Larry.

"Well," said Craig Kim, "whatever your idea is, it had better be a good one. Because if the coral reefs get inducted into ISIS, and ISIS does away with all of the imminent threats to coral reefs, then our species are both screwed. I mean, we're not killing them off directly like you guys are, but let's face it, we are kind of the jerks of the whole coral reef environment, so..."

"Well then, let's not let that happen," said Randy.

"Wait, you guys," said Larry. "If the coral reefs really are a species whose minds are vastly superior to ours, and who are helping the Earth rather than destroying it, and who have truly earned a place in the Intergalactic Society of Intelligent Species, then who are we to stop them? Shouldn't we just stand aside and let them have this, for the greater good of the Universe?"

There was silence as Randy and Craig Kim pondered Larry's deeply meaningful words.

"Guys! I'm just fucking with you!" Larry laughed. "Don't look so serious. Of course we're not gonna let some overhyped seaweed brain thing take this planet away from us. Freeeee-dooooooom!"

"Uhhhh...yeah..." said Randy. "Ok. Now, Craig Kim, let's talk about your mind control power and how exactly that works. Because the way I see it, here's what needs to happen..."

34. THE FINAL HOUR

"Why are we even here?" whispered Larry.

"Because obviously if The One just didn't show up at all, that would look pretty suspicious!" Randy whispered back.

They looked down at the massive crowd of strange life-forms amassed before the stage, then at their own supersized images on the enormous video screen behind them. It was the same stage within a giant floating bubble at the center of Atlantis where Jamiroquai and George Clinton had performed earlier. Someone gestured them toward their contestant podiums on one side of the stage.

"Alright then, everybody!" said their host, a green man in a funny hat. "It looks like we've arrived at tonight's...er, today's...you know, I never know what time it is down here!"

The audience laughed.

"In any case," the green man continued, "we've arrived at our main event, and I could not be more excited for this one. I'm your host, Osiris, Lord of the Underworld, and welcome to Cosmic IDOL!"

The crowd roared, and there was thunderous applause.

"As you know," Osiris continued, "we hold these events from time to time, across the known Universe, but this is only the thirty-third time that we've had one for the planet Earth."

"They've already done this thirty-two times without a winner?!" whispered Randy.

"That seems like a lot!" whispered Larry.

"And what a beautiful planet it is!" continued Osiris. "Of course most of us only know it from Atlantis, but let me tell you, if you ever get a chance to visit the surface...some of it is still habitable!"

The audience laughed.

"I don't get it," whispered Larry.

"Jokes aside, though," Osiris said, "that's pretty admirable for a planet with two potentially intelligent species at this stage in their development."

"Did he just call us—?" whispered Randy.

"Yep," whispered Larry.

"Speaking of which species," said Osiris, "Without further ado, let's meet our contestants!"

The audience went wild.

"On my left," said Osiris, "I have Randy and Larry, who, after several late lineup changes, appear to be our contestants for the species known as homo sapiens!"

The audience clapped and cheered.

"And slightly closer on my left, I have Craig Kim, an anthropomorphic manifestation of the ancient mindstream known as The Kraken, and Hachi the Octopus, representing the cephalopods!"

Larry looked more closely at the small octopus standing on top of the podium next to Craig Kim, both of whom were right next to Randy and him.

"Who the hell is Hachi the Octopus?" whispered Larry.

"Beats me," said Randy. "You'd think we would know that sort of thing."

"Right? I mean—"

"So! Randy and Larry!" said Osiris.

"Whuh?" replied Randy and Larry.

"I feel like you're a bit of a mystery to our audience, especially those who have been following the show for a long time. I'd like to get to know a little more about you. For example, what do you like to do in your spare time, when you're not training to be The One?"

"Ooh..." said Larry. "Just, you know. Regular human stuff."

"Totally," said Randy. "You know, just...humaning. Every

day I'm humanin', every day I'm humanin'. Am I right?"

There was an uncomfortably long silence.

"Ok!" replied Osiris. "The judges have ruled your response weird, but admissible! Now, Kraken and Hachi, I'd like to ask you..."

◆ ◆ ◆

"Ok, we made the switch. Now we need to haul ass out of here," said one of the Krak Babies, who was currently a host for Randy's mind. "Discreetly, of course."

"So let me get this straight," said another Krak Baby, who was actually Larry. "We just sent a fake version of a fake pair of contestants to a fake contest?"

"Something like that," said a third Krak Baby, whose gray matter was currently occupied by the Craig Kim thread of the Kraken mindstream. "But as we're going to need all of the mental resources we can get for our mission, I could only spare two sub-sub-sub-sub processes of the Kraken mindstream to occupy your bodies."

"So you're saying—?"

"They're a couple of idiots."

The three of them were walking quickly in unison with the rest of the Krak Babies, and nobody who saw them would have guessed that three of these things were not like the others.

"Hey Randy," said Krak Baby Larry, "remind me to shave my head like this when we get home. It feels so liberating!"

"Will do," said Krak Baby Randy. "So, Craig Kim, did you send a fake you to IDOL too, then?"

"No," said Krak Baby Craig Kim, "I just split my own primary mindstream between the Craig Kim body and this one, so that I can still answer intelligently. Just in case your girlfriend was tricking us again, or all of you are trying to trick me, and the Cosmic IDOL in Atlantis is not actually a fake."

"Oh, fuck off!" shouted Krak Baby Larry. "And you sent idiots to play us?"

"I thought it would be more convincing," Krak Baby Craig Kim laughed.

"Yeah, probably. Man, I hope that's not actually the real contest here at Atlantis, then."

"There's only one way to find out," said Krak Baby Craig Kim. "So, how are we getting to Sydney?"

"Oh, don't worry about that," said Krak Baby Larry. "We've got people."

"We do?" asked Krak Baby Randy.

"Well that's fantastic," said Krak Baby Craig Kim. "Because there's nothing more reliable than people."

"Awww, really? That's sweet of you to—"

"NO! Damn it, why doesn't the sarcasm ever come across when I'm speaking through these stupid kids? Fine. What I meant to convey, in literal terms, is that you human beings are an inherently unreliable species."

"Oh, yeah? Well...well...come at us!"

"You know, I'd rather just get to Sydney and maybe try to save both of our species from permanent extinction."

"Fine, then," said Krak Baby Larry. "You get us out of this subterranean shithole, and we'll get you to Sydney!"

"Fine!"

"Fine!"

Just then they all looked up and found a small crowd of humanoid adults staring at them and their Krak Baby squad.

"Do...do you children need any help finding your Mommy and Daddy?" asked one particularly concerned individual.

"Oh, fuck off!" replied Krak Baby Craig Kim. The adult's already strange face took on an expression of utter shock. "Oh, I'm sorry. Do you need any help with the fucking off?"

◆ ◆ ◆

"Now, we just have to find our way to one of the elevators before those idiots representing you guys say anything stupid enough to give us away," said Krak Baby Craig Kim, as they continued walking at a fast pace.

"Shoot, was anyone paying attention to the competition?" asked Krak Baby Randy.

Without breaking stride the Krak Babies all glanced up, at least insofar as the vacuous center of the Atlantis sphere could be considered 'up,' at the giant floating concert venue that was hosting Cosmic IDOL, with its massive video screen and speakers designed to serve the whole of the subterranean convention center.

"Randy, what do you consider to be the crowning achievement of your species so far?" Osiris was asking Fake Randy.

"Shit. Walk faster!" said Krak Baby Randy.

"Hey!" said Krak Baby Larry. "Why does your team have Hachi? I thought he was on our side, that lying bastard!"

"Oh, he was," said Krak Baby Craig Kim. "Until we kidnapped his family. That is, the ones who your people hadn't already kidnapped..."

"Ah ok, well I guess—"

"STOP!" shouted a familiar voice, and they all looked up toward the IDOL stage where it had come from. They saw Voltaire stumble onto the stage, bruised and battered, with his clothing hanging in tatters. "Stop zis charade at once! Zis man," he said, pointing an accusatory finger at Craig Kim, "is not a human!"

There was a brief pause.

"Correct, he's a cephalopod mind in human form," said Osiris. "Everybody here already knows that. That's why he's here competing for the cephalopod team."

"Uh...oh," said Voltaire. "So, like...oh. Huh. Ok, uh...carry on."

"STOP!" shouted another voice, this time directly in front of them.

Looking down from the overhead spectacle and back at their immediate surroundings, the Krak Babies discovered that they had nearly reached one of the many elevators that could take them to the outside. Unfortunately, between them and the elevator stood the human-sized forms of Yahweh and Cthulhu.

"AND JUST WHERE DO YOU CHILDREN THINK YOU'RE GOING?" asked Yahweh. Meanwhile Cthulhu just stood in front of them, looking as eldritch as ever.

"Well, shit," said Krak Baby Craig Kim.

35. GODS OF CHAOS

The Krak Babies looked at the two Ancient Ones standing directly in front of them.

"Doris, we're gonna need some help now," said Krak Baby Larry. "We need to get out of here and to Sydney, like pronto."

"Uhm...why are you talking to Doris?" asked Krak Baby Randy. "She's not here."

"I slipped her the tracking tag receiver from that shop in Tokyo, back in the UFO. And I've been putting the tags on pretty much everyone since then."

"Oh...I saw you wink at her but I thought it was just one of your creepy SugarMaby things so I wasn't going to ask any questions. Ok, so Doris can track our location, assuming she even knows what that thing even is, but can she hear us?"

"No idea. Guess we're about to find out."

Suddenly there was a flash of purple lightning off to their right, and they saw Randy's boss Frank appear.

"Hey guys," he said. "Doris said that you needed—"

With a soft WHOOSH a gigantic tentacle appeared from nowhere and grabbed Frank, then quickly disappeared with him behind a nearby building.

"Uh...Craig Kim? Did you happen to mention to your people that we're working together now?"

"It may have slipped my mind. My bad."

"Doris, we're gonna need some competent help now," said Krak Baby Larry.

There were a dozen or so purple flashes, and they recognized Gifford and his squad from the London office in full combat gear and armed with assault rifles.

"Alright, kids!" Gifford barked. "Facing me, away from the deities. Blink twice if you're Randy or Larry, three times if you're Craig Kim."

They followed his order.

"Good!" Gifford continued. "Now, these three kids are going to follow Simon out to the UFO."

Simon, the head of the London office, stepped out from behind some of Gifford's soldiers, wearing a full tuxedo and looking for all the world like James Bond. "Cheers," he said.

"And you, you, and you," Gifford continued, tapping several of the Krak Babies. "Will follow Delphine to the supersonic sub."

"Oh, hey Delphine," said Krak Baby Randy and Krak Baby Larry, just noticing that she was there, too.

"Hey, guys."

"The rest of you will go with these ninjas," said Gifford.

At which point they discovered the group of ninjas who had "rescued" them in Tokyo, who had now apparently rappelled down from...somewhere.

"We already told you, we're not ninjas," said the lead ninja.

"Right," said Gifford. "So, you guys follow the ninjas. My team will stay here and provide cover."

"YOU GUYS KNOW THAT WE CAN HEAR EVERYTHING YOU JUST SAID, RIGHT?" said Yahweh.

"We'll give you something to hear!" shouted Gifford, and his team began firing their automatic rifles in his direction.

"HA!" Yahweh shouted. "YOU'RE GOING TO NEED MORE THAN THOSE SMALL ARMS IF YOU WANT TO BOX WITH ME!"

And Cthulhu, who was receiving their fire as well, let out an eldritch roar.

Suddenly the two GODs began to grow larger, slowly at first, and then increasingly quickly, crumbling and knocking aside buildings and floating bubble structures as they grew, until it seemed that they took up the majority of the inside of

Atlantis. Aliens, neanderthals, and robots began to scream and scatter about frantically, no longer thinking about the IDOL competition.

The ninjas charged down a narrow alley and then out into a broader lane, several of the Krak Babies following close behind them. Far above, they saw the bubble containing the IDOL stage and video screen shatter, and the audience began to stampede and jump lemming-style out into the zero-g field surrounding it.

"Can you get us closer to that stage?" Krak Baby Craig Kim asked. "I've got an idea!"

They jumped off into low gravity and began climbing their way up the floating debris of the ancient architectural marvel that was Atlantis, the ninjas leading, and the kids following close behind.

"We're close enough," said Krak Baby Craig Kim. Perched on a marble column that was slowly rotating as it spiraled away from the core, he closed his eyes and concentrated. Randy and Larry felt a strange rush and became even more disoriented than they already were. Everything began spinning in circles and the cacophony surrounding them seemed to go silent for a brief moment. And then it all came crashing back to them as their vision resolved into a new perspective.

"What the hell just happened?" Larry asked.

Randy looked down at his own familiar body. "Hey," he said. "We're us again!"

"Exactly," said Craig Kim, who was floating in empty space right next to them. "I figure we're the last people they'll expect us to be."

"You!" said Larry. "Wait, are you you?"

"Yes," said Craig Kim. "I mean, I'm who I usually was before all of this. If that's what you mean."

"I don't even know what I mean anymore," said Larry. "Let's just go!"

They followed the ninjas back down among the ruined buildings and chaos, toward the inner surface of the sphere, until they finally touched down and gravity once again took hold of them.

Something exploded and sent the ninjas and Krak Babies scattering in different directions to avoid a falling stone wall.

In the chaos, one of the ninjas suddenly pulled Randy and Larry behind a half-destroyed bubble building and took off her mask.

"This is exactly why they keep those two locked up!" she grumbled.

"Takomi?" asked Larry.

"You're one of the ninjas, too?" asked Randy. "Wait, who do you even work for? The humans or the octopuses?"

"Goddamnit it's—wait, you actually said 'octopuses' correctly!"

"People can change," laughed Randy.

"Well," Takomi said, "I've actually been working for the humans and the octopuses at the same time. I figured it would give me my best odds after IDOL was finished."

"Smart," said Larry. "Hey, are you working for the coral reefs, too?"

"No," she replied.

"Well then, we should probably all get the hell out of here."

"Ah. Right."

They turned to run, when there was a purple flash of electricity directly in front of them.

"Uhm..." said Takomi. "What the hell?"

"Hey, sexy thang," said the newcomer, eyeing her up and down and not even attempting not to be super creepy about it.

"Aren't you on the hundred dollar bill?" asked Larry.

"Benjamin Franklin, at your service," the man replied. "Now step aside. Today looks like a good day for a deicide."

He lifted up a long iron rod, and with the flick of a switch there was a loud metallic clang as five razor-sharp prongs separated at the end of it.

"You like my Franklin Rod?" he asked Takomi with a

wink.

"Ugh," she replied.

Benjamin Franklin leapt out from behind the building, and as he disappeared from their view, they could see sputtering purple arcs of electricity shooting between the prongs of his rod.

"Huh," said Larry. "Well that was weird."

"Definitely weird," said Takomi. "Now let's get out of here."

"Right. But how are we going to get all the way to Sydney in time without getting captured?" asked Randy.

"If all goes well," Larry said, "Giffords's team will hold the GODs off long enough for the Krak Babies to get away. Delphine's team will get to the supersonic sub, which Cthulhu will go after. Simon's team will get to the UFO, which Yahweh will chase. They'll probably send some minions after the rest of the Krak Babies, who are still wandering around Atlantis looking like they're on some kind of mission. Meanwhile nobody will think to pay any attention to us and where we went. So we just need to sneak out, and get to Sydney really fast somehow."

"Cool," said Craig Kim. "How?"

"No idea. Unless…" said Larry, pausing for dramatic effect. "We didn't have to go all the way to Sydney."

❖ ❖ ❖

"What are you talking about?" asked Craig Kim. "And did you just pause for dramatic effect?"

"No!" said Larry. "Nobody does that! And what I'm talking about is a theory that I have."

"You," said Randy. "Have a theory."

"I can have a theory!" shouted Larry.

"Be my guest!" laughed Randy. "Theorize away, Pythagoras!"

"You're thinking of a theorem," said Craig Kim. "Go ahead, Larry."

"Well," said Larry. "We said the coral reefs are like 'Avatar.' And you know how in 'Avatar,' everything is sort of all connected together?"

"'Avatar,' most philosophies and world religions…" said Randy.

"So," Larry continued, "maybe instead of just each coral reef being a collective mind, what if all of the coral reefs in the world formed a mega collective mind together? Like, they can communicate between themselves somehow and they're all part of something larger."

"Yawn," said Randy.

"Interesting," said Craig Kim.

"Seriously?" said Randy. "We don't have time for this! We have to get to Sydney and stop the real IDOL!"

"It's not an entirely new theory," said Craig Kim. "In fact, many of the great cephalopod thinkers throughout history have entertained the idea. I myself spent some time researching the possibility, but in the end I could devise no way to determine if it was true."

"Who cares?" asked Randy. "What difference would it make for us anyway?"

"All of the difference," said Craig Kim. "We wouldn't need to go to the Great Barrier Reef, or any of the other reefs near Sydney where the real Cosmic IDOL might be taking place. All we would need would be any small reef…"

"What reef?" asked Randy. "Even if we manage to get back to the surface alive, we're in Switzerland!"

"Or an aquarium," said Larry.

"What?" asked Craig Kim.

"You know, like a saltwater reef aquarium," said Larry. "My buddy Unstable Pete had one back in the day. Bunch of coral formations in there and everything."

"Son of a bitch," said Craig Kim. "It's so crazy that it just might work."

"Guys," said Randy. "In real life nothing ever works if you have to say that."

"Shhh!" said Larry. "Listen to the thousands-of-years-old heffalump—"

"Cephalopod."

"Yes, that one. He said it might work, and it might work. And there's only one way to find out."

36. IN THE GARDEN

"Atlantis has a Chinese restaurant?" asked Randy.

"Everywhere has a Chinese restaurant," said Craig Kim. "We just have to get there."

"Won't they be closed?" asked Larry. "I mean, the world is ending and all."

"Chinese restaurants don't close. Sundays, holidays, end of the world. When did you ever see a Chinese restaurant closed?"

When they located the restaurant, they found that half of it was rubble and ash, and half of it was still standing.

"Welcome to Shambhala Garden," said the host at the door. "Table for three?"

"Yes," said Craig Kim. "As near to your fish tanks as possible. Your fish tanks are still intact?"

"Kitchen fish tank shattered by falling ceiling," said the host. "Dining room fish tanks are fine."

"Do they have coral?" asked Larry.

"You want to eat coral?"

"No, your fish tanks. That are still intact," said Craig Kim. "Do they contain live coral? We just want to look at the coral while we eat. We find it very relaxing."

"Ah, yes, coral," said the host. "Lots of coral, no problem. You eat, you relax. Don't worry about things falling from the sky outside. And maybe a little inside. Follow me, please."

Most of the diners had fled by now, their tables still covered with dishes of half-eaten food. The host walked them toward a table right next to a massive fish tank filled with a multitude of tropical fish, and plenty of colorful coral.

"Will this do?" he asked.

"Yes," said Craig Kim, "This will be just—"

"STOP RIGHT THERE!" came a booming voice. They looked up through the half-fallen ceiling and saw a gargantuan eye staring back down at them.

"Well that's unfortunate," said Randy.

"And...that would be Yahweh," said Craig Kim.

"Do you think he saw us?" asked Larry.

"That's literally his eye! There! Looking directly at us!" shouted Randy.

"Alright, geez."

"YOU THOUGHT YOUR PRIMITIVE RUSE WOULD WORK ON ME?"

"I'm sorry, what's a 'ruse?'" asked Larry.

"Just, like, a trick," whispered Randy.

"Then why doesn't he just say 'trick?'"

"I don't know!" Randy whisper-shouted. "He's God! He has to sound fancy! Oh, hey. Do you still have those smoke bombs from your cargo shorts?"

"Yeah. Why?"

"Because start chuckin' 'em around already, that's why!"

There were several pops, and the room suddenly filled with a thick smoke that obscured everything.

They only hesitated a moment, then the three of them scattered through a hole in the nearest wall and exited the restaurant. Only then could they see Yahweh towering in the air above them in his full resplendent glory.

Larry kept throwing smoke bombs.

"YOU WON'T ESCAPE FROM ME THAT EASILY!"

"Probably not!" Larry agreed.

"Hey, guys," said Craig Kim. "What is that up there?"

And indeed, somewhere far above Yahweh's head, in the chaotic vacuum of floating debris at the center of the Atlantis sphere, something was moving. Fast. It was too small to make out from the ground, but it ran like the wind and shot off purple sparks as it went. And then they heard the battle cry. Faintly at first, and then increasing in intensity as the tiny figure jumped from some platform high overhead and fell toward the very heart of their adversary.

"Leeerooooy Jeeeenkins!"

And they saw as he descended from the sky toward Yahweh, like Icarus in reverse, that it was Benjamin Franklin, but as he fell ever nearer, his Franklin Rod raised mightily over his head, as if to deliver a fatal blow to the universe itself, Yahweh's eyes suddenly glowed red, and without warning Benjamin Franklin burst into dazzling flame, and was instantaneously reduced to ash and ember. The Franklin Rod clattered to the floor unceremoniously, some distance from them.

"Well, shit," said Craig Kim.

Unable to locate them in all the smoke, Yahweh kicked an enormous sandaled foot in the direction of the restaurant, and managed to send one of the remaining sections of the dining room flying some dozens of yards away, where it crashed into another building, which crumbled and fell. The rest of the restaurant's ceiling began to come apart. A support beam fell and smashed into the fish tank with the coral, shattering the glass and spilling its live contents and salt water all over the restaurant floor.

"The coral!" cried Larry.

"I'll get it back into water!" shouted Craig Kim. "You two deal with him!"

"I feel like that's a really bad deal for us!" said Larry.

"Right? Does it really even need to be in water at this point?" asked Randy.

"WHERE ARE YOU LITTLE RODENTS?" asked Yahweh. He was stomping around, kicking at more buildings near the narrow alley where they were hidden.

"Psssst! Larry!" Randy whisper-yelled. "Go grab that Franklin Rod and throw it at him!"

"Ohhhh, no," said Larry. "My pastor would definitely not approve of that. You're the Atheist, you do it!"

"Seriously?" shouted Randy. "You're gonna play that card right now? You know I throw like a girl!"

"They're called *women!*" said Larry.

"No," said Randy. "I mean a little girl! And anyway, I'm an Agnostic!"

"Oh? What's the difference?"

"Well, you see the main thing is—"

"Guys!" shouted Craig Kim from inside what remained of the restaurant, his hands full of coral. "Can we focus?"

"Oh, suck it, Coral Boy!" shouted Randy. "Fine, I'll do this thing my own damn self! Larry, still got that explosive gel from your pocket stash?"

"I think so," said Larry. "Why?"

"Because start making shit blow up already!"

After a few moments, the explosions began all around them.

Randy made a mad dash for the Franklin Rod. He hesitated for a moment as he saw the purple electrical sparks shooting out of it, but knowing that there was nothing left to lose, he quickly grasped it in hand. It felt lighter than he'd expected, though it still had a nice heft to it.

"AH HA!" cried Yahweh. "THERE YOU ARE! AND I SEE THAT KALI'S WEIRD LITTLE BOYFRIEND HAS FOUND BEN FRANKLIN'S TOY. COME ON, LET'S SEE WHAT YOU'VE GOT!"

Randy lifted the Franklin Rod like a javelin. "Alright, then!" he shouted.

He paused for dramatic effect.

"Have it Yahweh!"

"Because, you know," Randy said, turning to Larry. "Like 'your way,' right? Yahweh. Your way. Was that at all—"

"Yeah, no, that one wasn't half bad, actually," said Larry. "Carry on."

"PASSABLE AT BEST," said Yahweh. "AND DID YOU PAUSE

FOR DRAMATIC EFFECT?"

"No!" shouted Randy. "Nobody does that! And besides—"

"You know," Larry interjected, "you should probably just throw that thing already."

"What?" cried Randy. "Oh. Right. This thing."

He pulled the Franklin Rod back, ran several paces like he'd seen them do once at the Olympics, and then with every last ounce of his physical strength and willpower, he launched it as high and as far as he could.

It was neither very high, nor very far.

"Ooh, that's not gonna make it," said Larry.

"HA!" said Yahweh.

"Well, shit," said Randy.

But by some miracle or stroke of luck, the Franklin Rod sailed just as far as the base of the enormous ancient deity who towered above them, and fell gently against the gargantuan small toe that protruded from the sandal on his left foot.

"WELL," said Yahweh, "SO MUCH FOR—"

But he stopped, as his left foot became suddenly engulfed in purple flashes of electrical lightning. He tried to shake it out, but the purple flames spread up his leg, around his torso in a spiral pattern, and soon enveloped his entire body.

"NOOOOOOOOOOOOOO!" shouted Yahweh.

And without further warning, he vanished into thin air.

"Uhm..." said Larry. "So, like, what just happened?"

"God is dead," said Randy, wiping the sweat from his brow. "And we have killed him."

"Dude. My pastor is so not going to be cool with this!"

"You can calm your tits, gentlemen," said Craig Kim, arriving conveniently just after the action. "You didn't kill anybody. You just sent him to another dimension. He'll find his way back before too long, and I'm guessing he's gonna be really pissed. So let's hurry up here."

They walked back around to the front of what little remained of the structure of the Chinese restaurant.

"Welcome to Shambhala Garden," said the host at the

door. "Table for three?"

"We were just—" stuttered Randy. "With the—I mean you must have seen—"

"Yes, please," said Craig Kim.

"This mapo tofu is delicious," said Larry.

"It really is," agreed Randy. "And this salted fish fried rice is incredible!"

"What?" Larry asked, seeing the look on Craig Kim's face. "The guy said we had to order something!"

"Indeed," sighed Craig Kim. "And it's all very tasty. But now we need to focus. I want you both to close your eyes. I'll need a few minutes to locate and understand the host minds we're trying to contact. In the meantime, I want you to remember what that crazy old man in London told you. Face your greatest weakness, and it will become your strength. Randy, what's your greatest weakness?"

"Uh...I don't know," said Randy weakly.

"Precisely," said Craig Kim. "You don't know. You don't know a lot of things, in fact. But you act like you do, because you want to seem smart. You have an intelligent mind, but you lack focus, and this leads you to learn a little about everything, and a lot about nothing. And you dress your lack of deeper knowledge in pretty words and concepts because you want to impress others. So, I'm going to go ahead and say that your weakness is pseudo-intellectual bullshit."

"Damn it, Craig Kim," said Randy.

"Cool," continued Craig Kim. "And you, Larry. What's your greatest weakness?"

"Beats me," said Larry. "I certainly don't go for all of Randy's pseudo-intellectual bullshit, I'll tell you that much."

"Oh, you don't indeed," agreed Craig Kim. "In fact, you eschew learning as a whole."

"I what learning?"

"Eschew," repeated Craig Kim.

"Bless you," said Larry.

"You also have an intelligent mind, but you lack trust in the experience and education of others outside of anything that has personally reached your own senses. You can call it 'street smarts' as opposed to 'book smarts,' or 'telling it like it is,' but I'll venture that your weakness is anti-intellectual bullshit."

"Fine," said Larry. "I'll play along. Can we just hurry up with this?"

"Ok. I've made the connection," said Craig Kim. "Now, I want you both to focus!"

"Wait," said Randy. "What about you? What's your greatest weakness?"

"That's easy," said Craig Kim with a sly grin. "I'm an insufferable douchebag with no actual friends who aren't manifestations of myself. We can use that, too. Now, let's all close our eyes and concentrate. Clear your minds..."

"Can I get you anything else?" asked their server.

"NOT NOW!" shouted Craig Kim. "Randy, think of the smartest thing that you've read lately. Or ever. That one work that made you wish you had written it. Pure poetry! Pure knowledge! Everything you could ever want to feed your mind! Now, more such works. More. More! Think of everything that you think a well-educated person should know!"

"And Larry!" he continued. "We don't need all of that bullshit Randy's thinking about! Think of the silliest pop-culture references that make you happy! Reality TV! 1980s cartoons! Sitcom trivia! It's all fair game!"

All of them remained completely still and transfixed, their eyes closed, no sensory stimulation apparently reaching them from the outside world.

"Uh...here's your bill, when you're ready," said their server.

"Oh, we're ready!" shouted Craig Kim. "Initiating transfer!"

37. REEFER MADNESS

"Yeah, it was really strange," said Kelli. "The coral reefs just kept babbling a bunch of nonsense about Nietzsche and Camus and the Kardashians, and calling everybody 'Bro.' The judges really didn't know what to make of it all. Word is, the reefs are going to be disqualified from Cosmic IDOL for at least the next several thousand years."

"Weird," said Randy.

"We definitely don't know anything about all of that," agreed Larry.

"So, your species will be spared from immediate and total annihilation," Kelli continued with a sly grin. "As will the octopuses. Lucky break for you all, I guess."

"Well, whatever serves the greater good," said Larry.

"So...what happens now?" asked Randy.

"Wait! Wait!" cried Larry. "I know this one! I've seen it a thousand times. This is where you employ the old memory wipe trope, right?"

"Uhm...well, yeah, actually," said Kelli. "There was a lot of damage done to Earth during this process and everyone has gone into an 'End of the World' furor, so we will in fact have to initiate a nano-level reconstruction process to put everything back in order, followed by a full-population memory wipe. Good guess!"

"Well, shit," said Larry. "I mean, I was actually just joking about the whole memory wipe trope thing. So, does that mean we're just going to go back to our old lives and forget that any of this ever happened?"

"Pretty much," said Kelli. "I mean, unless you're not located on the planet Earth when the memory wipe is activated."

"Not on the planet Earth?" Randy asked. "Where else would we be?"

"I don't know," said Kelli. "I hear the moons of Saturn are quite nice this time of year."

"Huh," said Larry. "And would you say that something like that might qualify as a date?"

"Yeah," said Kelli with a smile. "I think it might."

"Dude," said Larry. "Are you sure you want to go on a date with this chick? I mean, she's been playing you every which way over this whole Cosmic IDOL competition. I just don't want to see you get hurt."

"I know," said Randy. "And thanks. But look. I haven't had anything going on for a while. And if I start dating an alien from some advanced interstellar civilization, at least it's sure not to be boring! Seriously, after all that's happened here, how am I going to settle for some regular Earth girl?"

"Woman."

"Right. Woman. As for the lies, I don't think she had a lot of choice, it was all part of the job."

"Ok," said Larry. "I still don't like it, but just promise me this. You'll go in with your eyes wide open. Deal?"

"Deal," agreed Randy.

"So. You're, like, actually the goddess Kali?" Randy asked.

They were sitting on top of a rocky hill on Titan, watching the sun set over a vast hydrocarbon lake. Much of the cloudy reddish-orange sky was taken up by Saturn, with its spectacular rings. They sat inside some kind of invisible bubble with perfect air and temperature regulation, at least as far as Randy had understood.

Kelli laughed. "I guess," she said. "I think I'm most of the mother goddesses, actually."

"And how's that?"

"Kind of exhausting, to be honest."

"Wait, so how old are you?"

"You can't ask a woman how old she is!" Kelli laughed. "Anyway, I don't really remember anymore. Somewhere in the tens of thousands, at least. Is that weird?"

"Yeah, that's kind of weird," Randy said. "So we could get married and stay together for the rest of my life, and that would basically be a brief fling for you."

"Do you always ask girls to marry you, on the first date?"

"Hey, my life is short."

"It doesn't have to be, if I like you."

"Huh. Do you always offer guys immortality, on the first date?"

"They usually have it already. I mean, technically it's not true immortality, anyway. Just extreme longevity."

"Ok," said Randy. "So, I mean...why are you here?"

"It was a funny thing," Kelli said. "I fell in love with your TV, as a child. I mean, people watch Earth TV all over the universe. Everyone says they don't, or they say they're watching it for sociological purposes or whatever, but that's all bullshit. Anyway, I was top of my class at the Academy, and when it came to it, I could've deployed to pretty much anywhere I wanted. So, here I am!"

"I see," said Randy. "But what I meant was, why are you here? Now. With me. You're tens of thousands of years old and have all the knowledge of a super-advanced civilization. I must seem like some kind of trained monkey to you."

Kelli laughed. "You know we never really did get around to training you."

"No, I guess we didn't," said Randy. "I mean, it was a fake competition anyway. But I'd say we did ok."

"I'd say you did brilliantly! I mean, with my help, obviously."

"Just at the end. Why'd you give us those hints, anyway? I thought you were trying to keep us away from the real IDOL so the coral reefs could win."

"Well, sure," said Kelli. "That was my job assignment. Same with Yahweh and Cthulhu. But if I actually let that happen and ISIS eliminated the human species, then where would I get my TV from?"

"So, nothing to do with the crush that Cthulhu said you have on some human?"

Kelli grinned.

"Mostly the TV thing," she said. "Anyway, I had to be discreet because ISIS has eyes everywhere, but I was helping you from the start, you know. *Don't trust anyone, beware of false IDOLS*...how did you guys not connect the dots?!"

Randy's eyes opened wide. "You were the creepy old man?!"

"Guilty," Kelli laughed.

"And the weird survivalist shopkeeper in Tokyo!" Randy cried.

"Who? No, that wasn't me. Hey, is that where you guys got all that weird junk from?"

"Yeah, that was Larry. So, who else were you, then?"

"Nobody," Kelli said. "But I knew that Craig Kim was The Kraken, so I sort of planted the idea of kidnapping you two and then spying on our meeting."

"So we would know the truth before it was too late!"

"Right," said Kelli. "I said as much as I could in front of my colleagues, and I figured you guys could do the rest from there. As for your question about why I'm here, with you...I know what you mean. But think about it this way. If we took an ancient caveperson baby and put it in a modern Earth family, that kid would learn about your current level of science and technology just like any other kid, and use computers and the internet and all of that. In the same way, if you had been brought up on my planet, you would know the same things that I know. In fact, you still can. We're not born advanced as individuals,

217

we're just born into an advanced society."

"So you guys don't augment your minds with technology or something?" asked Randy.

"No, that's currently illegal under ISIS law as a subversion of the evolutionary process. This mind is au naturel, baby!"

"So if our minds are interchangeable and I could fit in fine in your society, then why are humans not being considered for ISIS membership?"

"Honestly?" said Kelli. "I don't know. I've been fighting the higher-ups on that point for millennia. It seems I see something in you that they don't."

"What do you see in me?"

"That was a plural 'you,'" said Kelli. "As in you all. Y'all."

"Ah, right. I knew that."

"Look," Kelli smiled. "You seem like a nice guy, you've got a curious mind, you're funny, and you're cute in your own quirky way. And you're not part of this whole ISIS thing, which frankly I'm pretty sick of. Plus, people really don't worship me much these days, and I guess I kind of missed it! Now, are you ever going to kiss me, or what?"

"Uh...ok," said Randy.

And he did.

"Well?" asked Larry. "How did it go?"

"Awesome," said Randy.

"Great," said Larry. "I mean, I still feel really uneasy about all of this, but I'm happy for you. So. Details!"

"I don't kiss and tell."

"Ok, so you kissed her..."

"Damn it! How did you crack that code?"

"Luck, I guess," said Larry. "Hey. There's something else that's been kind of bothering me."

"What's that?"

"Well, this funny metallic sphere with the squiggly blue

lights on it, from the shop in Tokyo. Everyone keeps telling me I'll know what to do with it when the time comes. But now here we are at the end of our little adventure, and we've sort of saved the world, and I still have no idea what the hell this thing is!"

"Yeah, good point. Why don't you go ask Kelli? She'll know what it is for sure."

◆ ◆ ◆

"Hey, Kelli?" said Larry.

"Yeah, what's up?" she asked, turning around. Her eyes opened wide when she saw the metallic sphere in Larry's hand. "Oh. Well, I guess I probably should have seen this coming."

"Seen what coming?"

"You're upset," said Kelli. "And you have every right to be. I lied to you and Randy."

"I mean, now that you bring it up, yeah," said Larry. "You didn't just lie to us. You used us as prawns in your crazy alien games!"

"Wait, did you say 'prawns?'"

"Yes."

"Oh, wow," she said. "Look, I'm really sorry. I did what I had to for my job. And I never thought things would go as far as they did with you two. I figured the octopuses would detain you —"

"Torture us..."

"Preferably not. Then the real IDOL would pass..."

"And our species would be annihilated?" laughed Larry. "Cool beans."

"I mean, I did help you stop that from happening, and—"

"Only because we screwed up your original plans by escaping prison, and then Craig Kim kidnapped us! You know what? I think Randy deserves better than you! There, I said it."

"Look," Kelli said. "I'm sorry for what I did. And I like Randy. I really do. I was honestly really looking forward to seeing where things might go."

She sighed.

"Where did you even get that memory wipe device, anyway?" she asked.

"Memory wipe dev- OH! Right, this memory wipe device that I'm holding in my hand right here," Larry said. "Obviously. Well, you know. I have people. So, like, how would one go about using something like this?"

"Look," said Kelli. "You got me, so you don't have to rub it in. Clearly you're going to alter my memory so that I think I'm a regular Earth woman with a regular Earth life, so that I can date Randy without all of this excess baggage, and you can sleep better at night."

"Uh...right," Larry said. "Of course. I mean, I would definitely like to sleep better at night. And I really can't see how I'm ever going to be ok with this situation as it currently stands. All of the lying and manipulation, and now you want to just go out with my best friend? I'm sorry, I don't think I can handle that."

"You know, go ahead," said Kelli. "You're right about one thing. Randy does deserve better. He's a really good guy. So go ahead, wipe my memory. Make me into an ordinary Earth girl, and maybe if I'm lucky he'll keep me around, and maybe for once in my life I might be a little bit happy!"

"Goddamnit," Larry sighed. "Do you really like him?"

"Yes."

"And he really likes you?"

"Seems that way. So go ahead. Wipe my memory."

"Uhm...Ok," said Larry. "Huh. Son of a bitch. It looks like I really do know what to do with it when the time comes. How about that? So, this is a little awkward, but how do I actually make this thing work?"

"The device employs an advanced artificial intelligence, so you don't have to do much. Just hold down the button, and tell it the outcome that you want, addressed to the target. Something like 'You will forget everything you know about ISIS, ORB, Cosmic IDOL, and life outside of the planet Earth...'"

Larry pushed the button and held it down. "You will forget everything you know about ISIS, ORB, Cosmic IDOL, and life outside of the planet Earth..."

"You were born on Earth, and have lived a very ordinary life," Kelli continued. Small tears formed in the corners of her eyes. "You will remember none of the extraordinary events that have taken place involving aliens, zombies, octopuses, ancient deities, etcetera etcetera."

"You were born on Earth," repeated Larry, "and have lived a very ordinary life. You will remember none of the extraordinary events that have taken place involving aliens, zombies, octopuses, ancient deities, etcetera etcetera."

"You are nothing but a normal Earth person," Kelli said, "and you care about Randy."

"You are nothing but a normal Earth person," Larry said, "and you care about Randy."

"Now you point this little sensor on the device at the target, and say 'Activate.'"

"And that's it?" asked Larry. "It's done?"

"That's it," confirmed Kelli. "And just so you know, you're a really good friend."

Larry sighed. "I know," he said.

He pointed the sensor on the metallic ball at his own forehead.

"Larry, what are you—"

"Activate," he said.

38. LOOKING AHEAD

"Foreshadowing," Larry said.

"See? I knew it would be Foreshadowing!" Randy laughed. "Didn't I tell you it would be Foreshadowing this week?"

"Uh...no," said Larry. "When did you even tell me that?"

"Right," said Randy. "No, I don't think I did, now that you mention it. I must have just thought it in my head."

"Weren't we just on forced exposition?" Larry asked. "And then it was supposed to be something with metaphors, but now Judy said we already did that and something else called deuces ex...I don't know. Are you guys as lost as I am?"

"Oh," said Kelli. "Uh...yeah, totally. I think Judy is just really disorganized, maybe."

"Yeah, I guess that's it," said Larry. "Anyway, I've been enjoying taking this class with you guys. I'm really glad Kelli suggested it."

"I...oh, yeah, I suggested it," said Kelli. "That sort of makes sense. You're welcome, then."

"You know, you guys make a great couple," said Larry. "This is stupid, but remind me again how you met?"

"Zumba!" said Kelli.

"Yoga!" said Randy, at the same time.

"It was, a, uh… zumba yoga workshop," said Kelli. "Very esoteric. And super trendy."

"Huh," said Larry. "You'll have to show me how that works."

"Alright, class," said Judy. "Thank you for your time and effort today. We'll see you again next week, to continue our study of my trademarked Eight Elements of Bad Writing. Our focus will be on the Exploitation of Dreams."

"Sounds ominous," said Larry.

"You know," said Kelli, "you two have had some pretty amazing adventures together. But somehow, some way, I feel like you still have many more great adventures to come."

"Are you still doing the foreshadowing exercise?" asked Larry. "You know class is over."

"I know," Kelli laughed. "So. What now?"

"Drink?" suggested Randy.

"Drink," said Larry.

"Drink," agreed Kelli. "Oh, hey, Larry. Maybe I'll invite my friend Delphine. She's recently separated and I feel like you two might get along."

"Sure, why not," said Larry. "Randy, didn't we meet a Delphine at your office Christmas party?"

"You know, I think that's her," said Randy.

"Huh," said Larry. "Small world."

"It really is," Randy said with a smile.

ACKNOWLEDGEMENTS

Thank you to all of my family and friends for putting up with my writing hobby.

Thank you to my early readers, especially Dad, Patricia, and Ben for the extensive feedback, which I made use of to the best of my ability.

Thank you to Duke Tran for the awesome cover art. (fiverr.com/trandinhnhanduc)

Thank you to Arthur C. Clarke, Harry Harrison, Michael Crichton, William Gibson, George Lucas, Rod Serling, and all the others who made me love science fiction.

Thank you to George Carlin, Chris Rock, the Monty Python crew, and everyone else who taught me the power of humor.

Thank you to the reader, for taking a chance on an unknown author. Hope you had a laugh or two.

ABOUT THE AUTHOR

Brent Mclean

Brent McLean has lived in California, Oregon, Washington, New York, Japan, and France. He's been a babysitter, an altar boy, a clothing salesman, a guy who plugs cables into a machine that goes beep, a computer programmer, a marketing account director, a sales account director, and a stay-at-home dad. Sometimes he writes stuff, after the kids are in bed.

WANT MORE RANDY & LARRY?

Thanks for reading! If you enjoyed this book (or if you didn't), I'd love to hear your thoughts in a review. Adding a review on Amazon is the #1 way to help more readers find the book.

For news and updates on future installments in the Randy & Larry series, and to chat about science fiction, geek humor, etc., check out
facebook.com/RandyAndLarry

Stay tuned for "Randy & Larry Dream Big," available whenever my kids let me get around to writing it.

Made in the USA
Columbia, SC
30 September 2020